THE OTHER VICTIM

A gripping crime thriller full of twists

HELEN H. DURRANT

JOFFE BOOKS

Published 2018 by Joffe Books, London.

www.joffebooks.com

This book is a work of fiction. Names, characters, businesses, organizations, places and events are either the product of the author's imagination or are used fictitiously. Any resemblance to actual persons, living or dead, events or locales is entirely coincidental. The spelling is British English.

ISBN- 978-1-78931-030-6

For all my wonderful readers — you know who you are.

Prologue

With its neat stone semis and manicured front lawns, Westgate was a quiet street. Tall oaks bordered the wide pavements and the only sound was the leaves rustling in the summer breeze. It looked like the perfect place to live.

"You'll have a good view of the hills from the back," Mavis Hartle said. "And you won't have far to go to the shops. Always a bonus that. And there's a bus stop on the next street that'll take you straight into Huddersfield centre."

Such details didn't bother her sister. At this point, Dawn Benson simply wanted to get the move over and done with. The moment she saw the house, she knew it was the one. She'd walked through it once and went straight back to Potter's estate agents and made an offer. With a bit of care and attention, it had the makings of her dream home. Today's viewing was simply about showing Mavis.

"There is plenty of room at the front for the extension. It'll make the sitting room so much bigger," Dawn was saying. "Then at the back, I'll have a conservatory overlooking the garden."

"That'll cost a bit, won't it? Don't overreach yourself, our Dawn," Mavis said.

"Let me worry about that. I've already submitted plans. Others on this street have had similar things done, so there shouldn't be a problem."

"I wish the agent would get here. He's taking his time." Mavis Hartle checked her watch. "The appointment to view was for two thirty. It's almost three now."

"He could be running late. Anyway, it's a nice day, and we're not in any rush. But you're right. I'll give the agents a ring. See what's happened to him." Dawn Benson tapped her foot impatiently as she waited for them to answer. "Hello," she said at last. "I'm on Westgate, waiting for Mr Potter. Is he on his way?"

"He left the office ages ago. He should be there by now. I'll call him on his mobile and ring you back."

"They're trying to find him," she told Mavis.

Dawn closed her eyes and soaked up the atmosphere. Somewhere nearby a dog barked, but that was all. No screaming kids, no lads kicking footballs at the cars. After the noise and bustle of where she lived now, this street was heaven. The ringtone of a mobile, somewhere close by, broke into her reverie.

"It's coming from inside." Mavis peered through the front window, walked round to the front door and gave it a gentle push. It swung open. "Come on, Dawn. Perhaps he's out the back."

The two women went inside. The place was still, silent and empty of furniture. The house had been let for several years, and the last tenant had already moved out.

"I'll try the back garden," Mavis said.

Dawn left the sitting room and walked into the kitchen. Everything was clean and freshly decorated. Her gaze went straight to the new modern units and the shiny marble worktops. She smiled. This was definitely the house for her.

The floor felt sticky under her feet. She looked down, and for a moment she was stunned. She couldn't believe what she was looking at. In an instant, all her hopes for the house and her life in it evaporated. Dawn felt the bile rise in her throat. The sight was horrific. The stone tiles of the floor were covered in a red fluid. And there, lying in his own blood, was the estate agent, Mr Potter.

Dawn steadied herself against one of the units, wanting to retch. Then she found her voice, and screamed out for her sister.

"He's dead," she whispered, and clutched Mavis's arm. "He's been murdered. There's a knife in his chest."

Chapter 1

Day 1

Superintendent Talbot Dyson took one look at the body on the trolley, raised his hands and backed away. "I'll leave you to it, Sid. Feeling a tad squeamish this morning."

It was the instruments that did it, cold, clinical, and neatly laid out ready for use. Doctor Sidney Bibby was in his scrubs, hat on and gloved up. Talbot shuddered. He must have attended hundreds of these over the years but it never got any better.

"Nonsense. You haven't got a squeamish bone in your body," Bibby said.

"Have today. Late night session, you know. My head's banging and my stomach's doing somersaults. Watching you cut this one up will make me throw."

"You should consider giving all that that up, a man your age. Losing a couple of stone wouldn't go amiss either."

Talbot rubbed his paunch and grinned. "Cheeky bugger! Do you know how long, and how much dosh it takes to get one like this?" He glanced at the body. "He looks familiar. Do we know 'im?"

"It's the estate agent. Ronald Potter, from Marsden."

"Wonder who he upset." Talbot took a quick look at the wound. "That bled some. Looks deep. What d'yer think, Sid?"

"He was a tall one, I'll tell you that. Six foot two. I've had a cursory look. From the track of the wound, I'd say he was got at like this." Sid Bibby put an arm around Talbot's ample waist and pretended to push a knife straight in, horizontally. "Had the assailant been smaller, the track would have been upwards, towards the heart," he speculated.

"Someone as tall as himself then? Narrows it down," Talbot said with a chuckle. "Can you tell me anything about the knife?"

"Large, wide blade, no serrated edge. The type you can buy for the kitchen, nothing special."

"Killer went prepared then."

"Who'll you put on this one?" Bibby asked.

"Brindle will be the SIO. He's back with us full-time, but I've got him some more help. We've got a new one starting this week. A woman DS from Central Manchester. Hope her face fits."

"Brindle settling in, is he?" Bibby said. "After what happened."

"He's doing fine. He'd be here now, but he's got a couple of days off. That place of his takes a lot of sorting. They opened up the house a couple of months ago but he's still not happy. I'm going to have to go and drag him away. That won't go down well with the fragrant Lady Evelyn."

"Do I continue then? Or do I put him on ice?" Bibby said.

Talbot went to the door and beckoned to a distinctly green DC Ian Beckwith. "You can get it done now, Sid.

Look and learn, lad," he said to Beckwith. "When it's over, you can report back to DI Brindle."

* * *

"*Blackpool comes to Brindle?* What on earth has possessed you, Matthew!"

Here it was, his mother's anticipated tirade of opposition regarding the event he'd organised on the Brindle estate. "It'll bring in the crowds," he said. "It's just what we need to put us on the map. We might be open, Ma, but we're not making a fraction of the income we need. This initiative will sort that."

"Initiative? Call it what it is, Matthew, a fairground. There'll be noisy rides and shrieking kids late into the night. We'll get no peace and it'll scare the wildlife, not to mention the animals on the farm."

Tutting, she left him in the doorway and went into the huge Georgian mansion. He followed her inside. "All the changes we've made didn't come cheap, you know. Setting up the farm, and converting the outbuildings have cost a fortune. Publicity isn't cheap either."

"It'll be a shambles, I know it will," she said. "Where will all the rides go? How will we cope with the numbers?"

Matt Brindle rolled his eyes. His mother was up on her high horse again. They had agreed months ago that the way forward was to open the house and grounds to the public, and that's what he'd done. But Lady Evelyn didn't like any of it. Her latest ploy was to resist everything he tried to do to bring in the crowds.

"Think about it, Ma," he said. "We can't go back to the way things were. Upkeep of the Brindle estate was bankrupting us. There was no way we could ever afford repairs to the place. This way, within a couple of years, we could have it done. We've already made good the west gable."

She ran a critical eye over his wiry frame. "You'll wear yourself out. The work, the worry. You've lost a lot of weight since you started this, Matthew. If you're not careful, you'll make yourself ill."

"I'm fine. The work is doing me good. After I was injured, I lay around the house piling it on, remember?"

"Perhaps if you spent more time here, running the enterprise yourself. Sarah does her best, but she isn't you. She doesn't have your drive. What with this and your job in CID . . . You're torn between the two. I know what you're trying to do with the estate, son. Deep down, I know it is the only way. But the enterprise needs you full-time."

Small consolation, but was she right? He had worked hard over the last few months, and despite feeling the strain, it had paid off. Today, the main rooms of the house were open to the public. They had a well-stocked petting farm that was proving popular. The café and the gift shop did good trade too. All as he had originally planned. Matt didn't consider that his work in the police got in the way, but he was also realistic. The Brindle estate was demanding and would continue to be so. His current initiative was about bringing in the numbers. Not enough folk knew about the place yet. That would happen in time, sure, but the financial pressure was such that they couldn't wait.

"The event will be held on the south field by the lake," he said firmly. "The press release has already gone out. Like it not, Ma, we're committed."

She wasn't listening. Her eyes were on the view from the window. "There's a car coming up the drive, looks like Talbot. Doesn't he know that you've got time off?"

She was angry at the super's sudden appearance, he knew, but there was nothing he could do. He had gone back to CID, his choice. He also knew that he needed time off to see to the estate, but this was something of a luxury. If only his mother would open her eyes and see things as they were. He sighed and, leaving her to it, he went to meet the superintendent.

He smiled at Talbot. "Missing me already?"

"I know you've got leave, lad, but we've got a body. I don't want to give it to Carlisle, he's got plenty on of his own."

"What's happened?"

"Do you know the estate agent from Marsden, Ronald Potter? Well someone's stuck a bloody big knife in him. Frightened a couple of prospective buyers to death."

Matt looked towards the café building. His sister, Sarah, was working up there. He should tell her. "Go inside, have a cuppa with Ma. See if you can cheer her up, she's been banging on about the house again. I'll just speak to Sarah and then I'll join you in a minute."

Chapter 2

The girl was crying, banging on the stone wall with her bare hands for attention. She had no idea how long she'd been locked up. There was a noise upstairs. Someone was walking about, and that meant her captor was back. She screamed out, but there was no response. No one would come. She sank to the floor. What was the use? There was no way out of here.

The girl couldn't remember what had happened before waking up in this cold, dark space. She'd been drugged, her aching head told her that much. She'd been injured too. She couldn't see the wound, but her right calf hurt like hell whenever she moved.

She was imprisoned in a small dark room, possibly a cellar. She'd felt her way all around the walls, and there was only one door which was securely locked. Her captor had left a bottle of water. From time to time she was given food, sandwiches mainly, nothing hot. To sleep on, she'd been given a camp bed and a smelly old quilt.

The girl tried banging again. She was fastened to one wall by a long chain. She bunched up several links and used them to hammer on the door.

An angry voice called down the cellar steps. "Shut it! I told you, no one's coming. You're not going anywhere. You know the deal. Make yourself comfortable, 'cause you'll be here for a while."

The girl began to sob all over again. "You can't do this!" she screamed. "Please . . . please, just let me go. I won't say anything." She closed her eyes and waited. Nothing. Her captor was not going to release her.

Another flashback, they were getting more frequent. Her memory was returning. She'd been walking down a path, going to see someone. The girl suddenly remembered that she'd come to this house herself, willingly. There must have been a reason, but she couldn't remember what it could be. She'd met her captor, and the two of them had talked. They'd even shared a joke. She remembered laughing at one point. The room they were in was pleasant, with a view of the garden. She'd been happy to be here.

The girl closed her eyes in an effort to remember more. There had been photographs and ornaments on the mantelpiece above a huge ornate fireplace. She had picked up an old photo in a frame. Her captor had flown at her angrily. That was when her leg had been injured. Her captor had grabbed hold of a poker, lashed out at her lower leg, and had laughed, said it served her right. The girl rubbed her leg. The wound had bled. It was bandaged, but it ached and didn't feel right.

Why was she here? What made her so important? As far as she could remember, she'd come here because of a job. One thing was for sure, there was no way out. She felt sick.

* * *

Matt Brindle arranged for DC Lily Haines to meet him outside Potter's Estate Agents in Marsden. It was mid-afternoon, but the agents weren't busy. A woman of around forty sat at a desk in the office, smartly dressed in a dark, fitted suit and heels. She was not unattractive but wore too much makeup. She greeted Matt and DC Haines with a practised smile. She obviously didn't know what had happened.

"We're from East Pennine CID." Matt showed her his badge. "You work here?"

"I'm Mary Salter, employee, general dogsbody, friend, and one-time partner." The woman lowered her eyes when she admitted to that one. "Why, what's happened? Where *is* Ronald?" Her gaze moved warily from one detective to the other.

There was no easy way to say this. "I'm afraid Mr Potter has been murdered. He was found this afternoon at a house he'd arranged to show to a prospective buyer."

Her face fell. "The one on Westgate? Pity. The sale is practically complete. Not anymore, I'll bet. Despite all her grand plans, Dawn Benson is bound to pull out now. Who'd want to live where a murder took place? Folk won't forget either. I doubt it'll even let after this. Shame, the business needs the money."

"Grand plans?" Matt queried.

"A big extension to the front, a sunroom to the rear. The woman must have money to burn. She'd already spoken to the planning department. Apparently a cousin of hers works there."

Not a mention of what had happened to Potter. Hadn't it sunk in? Didn't this woman feel anything at all? "We're having difficulty finding a family member to identify him," Matt said. "We were hoping you could help us trace them."

"He has no one. I'll do it," she said. Still not a flicker.

"If you're sure. It isn't a pleasant job."

"I worked with Ronald for ten years. There's no one else, so it's down to me."

"It can wait until tomorrow," Matt assured her. "I'll send someone in the morning to take you to the morgue. In the meantime, we need to know about Mr Potter's life, who he was friendly with, if he had any enemies."

"He had very few friends — too abrasive, you see. I did tell him. Ronald, I'd say, you need to start treating folk better. It's not good for the business, all that attitude."

"You're saying that he could have had enemies?"

"No one that would want to kill him. He was a bit sharp at times, that's all." She put a hand on her forehead. "It's hitting home now, this news. I'm beginning to feel quite woozy. I think I'm going to have to lock up and leave early."

"Does he have an appointments diary?" Lily asked. "It might help to know who he saw recently."

Mary Salter took it from the desk and handed it over. "There's not a lot in it for the last few months. Trade was slack. The rental market was brisk, but not sales. I know it worried Ronald. I'll miss him and his odd little ways. I don't suppose I'll have a job for much longer either."

"Who owned the property on Westgate?" Lily asked.

"One Andrew Kent. He and Ronald knew each other. They went to school together. Kent lives in Spain, and he's never actually seen the place. He owns half a dozen houses in the area, and Westgate is just another property in his portfolio. He's had that one for the last twenty years. Up until recently, they've all been let out. He got in touch with Ronald about a month ago, said he needed to raise some money, and to sell one. He left it up to Ronald to make the decision and see to the details. Westgate was the one most likely to sell fast. The tenant had given notice. Shame, all that has been put on hold now. As I said, Dawn Benson, the buyer we had lined up, is sure to pull out. Can't say I blame her."

"Mr Potter lived upstairs. Do you have a key?" Matt asked. "We'd like to take a look around. My colleague and I, plus scenes of crime people, will come tomorrow and search the flat properly."

"I'm afraid I don't. It was probably in his pocket. Why? What do you expect to find? He led a very simple life, did Ronald. Far too simple, if you ask me. He must have made a lot of money over the years, but he did nothing with it."

* * *

Back at the station, Matt sat at his desk scrutinising Ronald Potter's work diary. The man was meticulous. Every viewing and its outcome was listed. What was missing, though, was information about his personal life.

"These are all very well, but we need to know about the man himself, not what he did to earn his living."

Lily Haines looked up from her desk. "He lived alone, didn't mix much according to that woman he worked with. As for living above the office, that surprised me. A man like him, into property and all that. You'd have thought he'd have got himself sorted. What did you make of her, the Salter woman?"

"A cold fish. She appeared to be more concerned about the loss of a sale and her job than about Potter. We'll have to speak to the neighbours. Push Mary Salter on the subject of friends."

Lily looked up. "He drank in the Weavers' Arms. I've seen him in there a few times, but always on his own."

Matt picked up the phone and dialled the morgue. Doctor Bibby would have done the PM by now, and he wanted to know if he'd found anything interesting.

"Apart from the knife wound, there's nothing, Matt. No defence wounds, nothing. In my opinion, he was taken by surprise. I've given a copy of my initial report to Beckwith. He has instructions to hand it to you."

"Any chance of DNA?"

"We'll test his clothing and body for foreign DNA. The good news is that we've got a good set of prints off the knife, and they don't belong to Potter. The bad news is that there's no match on the database."

"Did you find a key in any of his pockets?"

"Yes. Once forensics have done with it, I'll send it over."

Chapter 3

Day 2

A black eye. A real shiner, and no amount of makeup was going to make it disappear. Damn Zane and his temper. Kate Baxter donned a pair of sunglasses. Okay, it was August, but it was raining. She looked ridiculous.

"Soz, sis." Her brother, Zane came up behind her and peered in the mirror. He ran a hand through his dishevelled hair, yawned, and then limped off in the direction of the kitchen.

"You're a bloody liability, you are! I start a new job this morning. What are they going to think?"

He shrugged. "Never bothered you before. Tough it out. You're good at that."

"You were blind drunk again. You have to stop this, Zane."

"Life's for enjoying, sis. I'm making the most of it. I'm not a workaholic like you."

Kate watched him lower his skinny frame into the sofa, a dish of cereal in his hand. He was wearing pyjama bottoms, and was naked from the waist up.

"If you weren't my brother . . ."

"Baby brother too, don't forget." He had a big grin on his face. He knew exactly which buttons to press.

With everyone else, Kate had a reputation for being hard, uncompromising. But with the two people she was closest to, her brother and her mother, she displayed her softer side. Both were difficult to handle, and both took advantage. Zane had little respect for the law, or her place in it. Their mother had early-onset dementia and was in a care home. For as long as she could remember, Kate had managed to keep them in the background. No one at her old nick had ever met either of them. A sad state of affairs. She was thirty-two years old, and painfully embarrassed about her nearest and dearest.

"What have you done to your foot?" she asked.

"Got into a fight down by the arches. Those under that bloody big bypass out of Huddersfield. Think one of the scroats must have kicked me."

"Were you scoring drugs again?"

Zane shook his head.

"Then why go there? It's dangerous. It's where the dregs of this town hang out."

"Exactly!" He gave her another grin.

Kate flicked a rolled-up tea towel at him. "Don't be such an idiot. One of these nights, you'll meet the wrong person."

"I'm writing an article. I'm hopeful that the local rag will take it. I met the editor in the pub last week. He's looking for something current and edgy. A piece about the town's homeless and druggies should do nicely. If he prints it, I'm on my way."

"You'd do better going back to uni," she said. "You didn't give it long enough."

"Long enough for me, sis. That place was the pits."

Before she could reply, Kate's mobile rang. It was an unknown number.

"Ma'am," said the caller. "This is DC Haines from East Pennine CID. We have a body, a murder victim, discovered yesterday in an empty house. DI Brindle has asked if you could meet us at the victim's flat in Marsden."

Kate noted the woman's Yorkshire accent. "Text me the postcode. I'll be with you shortly."

This was it. She was off and running. She grabbed her jacket and bag. "Don't leave the house. I will not allow you to balls up this job for me, like you did the last one."

"No can do, sis. I'm seeing someone later."

"Not before we have a serious talk."

All she got in return was a shrug. Bloody fool! He needed to straighten himself out.

Living and working in Yorkshire was a complete change for Kate Baxter. She had been born in a small, red-brick terrace in Ardwick, on the outskirts of Manchester, and worked at the local station. If things had worked out differently, she would never have left. But family problems made staying in her old job difficult. Zane, her brother, had a habit of getting himself involved with the wrong people, and her colleagues had begun to notice. He'd never been officially questioned or cautioned, but his name came up frequently. The super at her old station noticed and had mentioned it several times. Kate had had enough. One day Zane's antics would seriously threaten her career. What was needed was a complete change, a fresh start somewhere no one knew them.

Zane Baxter had been a difficult child, wilful and disobedient. With their father dead and their mother in a home, Zane lived with his big sister. The problem was, Kate was no parent. She couldn't give him the time he needed to straighten himself out. She was a copper, a detective sergeant, and worked hard. She hoped to make DI within the next couple of years. When she was engrossed in a case, everything and everyone in her life took a back seat.

* * *

Matt Brindle and Lily Haines were searching Ronald Potter's flat above the estate agency on Marsden High Street.

Lily looked out of the front window at the passing traffic. The road outside was a through route to Huddersfield, and very busy. "Even my gaff is better situated than this."

"And all his furniture is well worn. He hasn't spent any money on this place in years," Matt observed. "Go through those drawers. We're looking for letters, documents, even photographs. We seriously need a handle on this man's life if we are to get who killed him. I thought the new DS was joining us?"

"I rang her earlier, and told her where we'd be." Lily took another look out of the window. "I think this might be her now. A woman has just parked up across the road. Have you met her?"

"No, but Talbot says she's okay. Hope she's up to it. First case, a murder, and no clues as yet."

It was a hard ask, but that was often the way of the job. It had been the same when he'd started back. He went straight into the thick of it, and there'd been no time to draw breath.

"Could the killing have been random?" Lily asked. "A burglar perhaps, chancing his luck?"

"The house was empty. There was nothing to take. No mess either. According to CSI, none of the locks were forced. No, I think Potter was targeted for some reason."

Lily went into the kitchen and sorted through the crockery and cutlery. There was one of everything. "He didn't entertain. He doesn't have the resources."

Matt stood in the centre of the sitting room, thinking. "This place makes me think that Potter was hiding something."

"What do you mean?"

"It looks like a bolt hole, a front. We'll take a close look at his finances, but a business like his, I bet he has money stashed away."

Lily held up a bunch of letters. "I found these in the drawers."

"Bag them and we'll have a look back at the station."

"There are also a number of bills and his old work diaries," she said. "And that's it."

Matt's attention was drawn to the mantelpiece. In the centre was a small picture frame, containing the image of a young woman. "I wonder who this is."

"We could ask Mary Salter. She's still working downstairs."

"Good idea. I think we're done here," Matt said.

They heard a knock at the door.

"Come in!" Matt called.

A strange woman walked in. "DS Kate Baxter."

"Hi." Lily held out a hand, which Kate ignored. "DC Haines."

"And I'm DI Matt Brindle, the SIO on this case. Welcome to the team." Matt smiled.

"What have we got?"

Short and businesslike, Matt noted. No pleasantries. "A body, belonging to the estate agent that owned this business, and not much else," he said.

"Motive?"

Lily looked up from searching the drawers. "Not yet. I'm Lily, by the way. We spoke on the phone earlier." She tried another smile. Like the first one, it was not reciprocated.

"This is where the victim lived," Matt said. "He was killed while waiting to show a client around a property a short distance from here. What do you think?" He stepped back to allow her to take a good look at the place.

"There's supposed to be money in selling houses, but this guy lived like a pauper. The furniture, even the cushions on that sofa," Kate pointed at them, "everything in here has seen better days."

"That's what I think too," Matt said. "Something isn't right here. We need to know what, and quick. We are about to have another word with the secretary downstairs. It'd be useful to get your take on her."

Kate Baxter was tall and thin with long red hair tied back in a ponytail. She hadn't smiled once and kept all talk minimal and to the point. Her clothing was casual, jeans and short jacket, a bit like Lily's. She didn't appear to be the friendliest of colleagues, but then they hardly knew her. Time would tell. Hopefully she'd mellow. She led the way down.

Mary Salter was sipping tea at her desk. "You might have warned me," she complained. "I've never seen a dead body before. It didn't look like Ronald at all."

"But it was him?" Matt queried.

"Oh yes, no doubt. He just, well, he looked different, that's all."

"Are you alright?" Lily asked. "Can we get someone for you?"

"I'm fine, love. I'll sort some stuff out here, and then I'll get off home."

"Do you recognise this woman?" Matt showed her the picture.

"That's Francine. She and Ronald used to be married."

Matt and Lily looked at each other. "We asked about Potter's family yesterday, but you didn't mention her," Matt said.

Kate moved forward. "Why was that?" Her voice was clipped and accusing. "I would have said it was vital information. What are you trying to hide?"

Mary Salter looked at Matt, not Kate. "Nothing! He'd just told me that Ronald was dead. I was in shock. Besides, Francine is easy to forget. Him and her didn't last two minutes. She was far too young for him."

"Where is she now?" Kate asked.

"No idea. Before she married Ronald, she lived in Holmfirth. Her parents are still there. She might be with them. Her maiden name was Earnshaw."

"Is there anything else you might have forgotten to tell us about Ronald, Miss Salter?" Matt asked.

The woman shook her head. "We might have gone out a few times, but he kept things close. Secretive — you know the type. I used to ask him questions but never got any answers."

"Does anyone else work here?" Lily asked.

"We have a part-time girl, Julie Powell. She does the odd afternoon when we're busy."

"Was she here yesterday?" Lily said.

"For a couple of hours."

Matt gave her his card. "Ring me if anything else occurs to you. By the way, do you know if he left a will?"

"He used Harcourt's, the solicitors in Huddersfield. They'll know."

They left her rifling through the papers on her desk.

Outside, Lily asked, "What now?"

"It's obvious." Kate spoke as if to a child. "The solicitor. I suggest you go and have a word with him, sir. I'll go after the ex-wife."

"No," Matt said firmly. "Kate, you can come with me. We'll speak to the solicitor together. If Potter did leave a will, he can tell us who inherits. After that we'll find Francine. Lily, you go back to the station and look through that little lot." He nodded at the bag of documents she was clutching.

"It would be quicker if we took a task each, sir," Kate said.

Matt looked at her. The woman was keen, there was no doubt of that. But the few minutes he'd spent with her had been enough for him to recognise the type. Kate Baxter was a woman on a mission. She'd have a plan. It would include rapid promotion, and God help her colleagues if they got in the way.

Chapter 4

Pamela Ansel, manager of the Huddersfield hostel for homeless women, regarded the woman who stood in front of her. "Have you told the police about your Kaz, Christine?"

Christine Fletcher turned aside from Pamela's accusing gaze. She was worried, tired, no doubt from lack of sleep caused by having to care for the infant she held in her arms.

"What good would that do?" she said. "They'll say our Kaz has run away again. That she'll come home eventually, like she usually does."

"And they could well be right, but I think you should go down to the station and report her missing anyway. I know your Kaz is a hothead, but she should consider the effect of her actions on others. Leaving you with the babe to look after is not on. You've got enough on your plate. How is Caleb these days? Managing to keep out of harm's way, is he?"

"Caleb has learned how to keep his nose clean. About bloody time. But Kaz expects too much from me. Our Kian's a lovely kid but he cries and I can't cope. I didn't cope well with Kaz either, which is why she ended up in care. I don't want the same for him. He's her kid, and she should be the one caring for him. If she doesn't come back, it'll have to be Social Services."

Pamela Ansel shook her head. "I'm sure you're doing a grand job with both Kaz and Kian. My advice is to stick it out. It'll be worth it in the end."

"I told you, I'm not coping. I don't have the patience. Our Caleb is no help with the babe. I know Kaz is a teenager with all the problems that comes with that, but neither of them gives a stuff about me. I don't need the strain. There's no bloke to take up the slack. I was hoping I'd find her here."

"We haven't seen her in weeks, Christine. Not since she got settled with you. Have you tried the other homeless hostels?"

"She wouldn't go anywhere else. You only take women. She trusts you."

Pamela Ansel knew Christine Fletcher of old, and had little sympathy with her. She was always looking for the easy way out. The infant would be cramping her style, keeping her in nights. She'd want Kaz back so she could palm him off on her. "I'd like to help you, Christine, but I can't. If Kaz does come here, I'll tell her to contact you. Does she have a mobile?"

"Course she does. She's never off the bloody thing. But she didn't have it with her when she left. It's still in her room."

"Tell the police, Christine. Something might have happened to her."

Christine Fletcher swore, bundled the infant into his pram and left.

An inmate who happened to be walking past eyed Pamela with curiosity, "She didn't look happy."

"She isn't, Tina. Her daughter is missing. Shame, I hope nothing has happened to her. She's a pretty girl. But it's none of your business, you know."

Pamela Ansel hated having to deal with the pretty ones. They always came off worst on the streets. Those and the spoilt brats who reckoned their parents did their stupid heads in and fancied living away from home. A row over something and nothing and they'd flounce out of the house, swearing they could go it alone. They had no idea. Life on the streets was no picnic. Pretty, and you ended up hooked on drugs and being pimped out by a dealer. Throw in spoilt, and you didn't survive long enough to know what hit you. In this area, the really unlucky ones ended up with Pamela.

* * *

They found Harcourt's solicitors on the top floor of an impressive Victorian building opposite the Huddersfield railway station. Jacob Harcourt ushered Matt and Kate into his office and offered them a seat.

"We've been seeing to Ronald's affairs for years now. Being in the business he was, he sent a lot of conveyancing work our way. I was sorry to hear of his death. A particularly unpleasant way to go, from all accounts."

"I'm trying to build a picture of the man," Matt said. "The way he lived, who he knew, if he had any close relationships, particularly any he may have made recently."

Harcourt looked perplexed. "I'm afraid I have no idea. We spoke on the phone a lot, but mostly about business. We'd have a drink from time to time, but that was about it."

"Didn't you discuss personal matters on those occasions?" asked Kate.

"Not really. Ronald wasn't an easy person to know."

"Did he leave a will?" Matt asked.

"Yes, he did. It's a very simple affair. He's left everything to his son, Daniel."

That came as a surprise. "I'd no idea he had a son. Mary Salter, Ronald's secretary, didn't mention him." Matt wondered why she was being deliberately frugal with what she told them.

"He wasn't married to Francine for long, but it was long enough to conceive Daniel," Harcourt explained. "He was Ronald's pride and joy. Mary Salter is jealous. She's always had eyes for Ronald. I'm convinced it wasn't the man that interested her, so much as the business. Ronald told me so himself. He was sure that was the reason she started a relationship with him."

"She did admit that they'd been seeing each other."

"Ronald wasn't interested. Francine refused to have him back, but there was no way he would get involved with a woman again in case it jeopardised his son's inheritance."

"The lad gets the business?"

"He does, plus the house and a sizeable amount of money. Ronald knew the business, and did well out of it. The lad and his mother live in Meltham. Ronald bought the house new and paid cash, plus all the expenses. Anything Francine needed for the boy, he provided without argument."

"What's her address?"

"Marle Crescent, number fifty. Daniel and Francine have lived there since she and Ronald split up."

"Is the business worth much?" Kate asked.

"Without Ronald's touch, I shouldn't think so. The premises are rented. I shouldn't think Francine will keep it on. The big boys, the online ones, are taking over the housing business these days."

Now they had an address for Francine Potter, so that was their next call.

"He thought the secretary had a thing for Potter. Did she give you that impression?" Kate asked when they were outside.

"No. Apart from admitting to the brief fling, I found her rather unconcerned about Potter's death."

"Is she a suspect then?"

"Not yet. We haven't got sufficient information to pin that on anyone so far."

* * *

The house on Marle Crescent was a large detached building. There was a red sports car in the drive and they could hear music playing through an open front window. It looked like Francine Potter was at home. The house next door was for sale. Matt noticed it wasn't being handled by Potter's firm.

Kate rang the bell. The woman who answered was young and pretty. Francine Potter looked no older than her mid-twenties. Tall, with shoulder length blonde hair, she was not what Matt was expecting. She had to have married Ronald for money — nothing else made any sense.

Francine scanned the two of them up and down through shrewd blue eyes. "I know why you're here. It's about Ronald. He's finally carked it, hasn't he? I heard something on the radio."

"He was murdered, Francine," Matt said sharply. "And it wasn't pleasant. We'd like to ask you some questions. We'll start with when you saw him last."

"I didn't kill the daft sod, if that's what you think." She sounded annoyed. "He sees our son every week. He doesn't come here, and we don't go to that tip he calls a flat. We usually meet in one of those soft play places. The last time was a fortnight ago. The little one's had a cold, so we missed a week."

Matt could see the boy hiding behind his mother's legs. He was still a toddler — about three, Matt reckoned. The upkeep of this house plus Francine and her son would be the reason Ronald had lived so simply. He was trying to save as much as he could for his son's future.

"Do you know who Ronald spent time with? Who his friends were?"

"He wasn't a mixer. A pint in the local, and then home. He preferred his own company. Basically, he was boring. The man was no fun. I got sick of telling him. He didn't have a laugh in him." She put her hands on her hips and stared at them. "I know what you're both thinking. I married him for his money, for the house. Well, you're right, I did. We went out for a while, and I got pregnant. I insisted on a ring and a ceremony for the sake of the child. I didn't love him and I made no secret of it. As for who else Ronald knew, I've no idea. You'd be better off asking that woman in his office. She must have known him far better than me."

"Can you think of anyone who wished him harm?" Kate asked.

"He had a bad temper. He got on folks' nerves with his prattle, but murder is going a bit far. He was just an ordinary bloke, nothing special."

"When you got married, did you meet any of his family?"

"He had an old aunt who lived Barnsley way. He told me that she died. I'm not aware of anyone else. When is the will being sorted?"

"I've no idea," Matt told her. "I'm sure Ronald's solicitor will be in touch.

"Think I'll give him a ring. He needs to hurry things up. Without the money Ronald provides each week, we'll go short."

Matt handed her his card. "Give me a call if you remember anything else."

They left Francine Potter to it.

"She's a piece of work," Kate decided. "All she's concerned about is the money."

"And all that concerns us, Kate, is whether she killed him."

"I don't think so," Kate said. "Potter was her meal ticket. Why spoil a good deal?" They got in the car. "Where to now?"

"Back to the station. We'll check in with Lily. See if she's discovered anything in our absence."

"You think that likely? She's very young, no older than that one in there. How much experience can she have?"

Her comment took Matt by surprise. He'd no idea what DS Baxter's game was, but he'd have to put her straight. "DC Haines might be young but she's good at her job. And she has plenty of experience. She's worked with me for several months and I've never found her wanting. We have honed a good working relationship." He didn't start the engine. Instead, he turned to face the new DS. "I hope that we can do the same. You, me and Lily, we're a team now. The most important word in that sentence, Kate, being *team*. Do I make myself clear?"

"That's me told. Sorry, but I speak as I find. A trait I was told you Yorkshire folk understood."

"What happened to your eye?" Her attempts to cover the bruise with makeup hadn't been successful.

She gave an unconvincing chuckle. "An argument with a cupboard door. I don't usually look like this. It's just unfortunate that it happened yesterday."

Matt guessed she was lying, but he didn't push it. He could only hope that Kate Baxter took on board what he'd said and settled in quick.

Chapter 5

"There's nothing of interest in the letters. Not that I can see anyway," Lily said. "They're mainly from an aunt, and they stopped coming about a year ago. The bills are old utility ones. The diaries follow the same pattern as his current one. Basically, it adds up to a big fat nothing."

"He had a son," Matt announced. "He and his mother, Ronald's ex-wife Francine, live in Meltham. We've just had a word with her. She wasn't very helpful and she admitted there was no love between them, on her side at least."

"The kid inherits?"

"Yes, and it's a sizeable amount according to the solicitor." He pointed to an empty desk. "Make yourself at home, Kate. This is our base. Tea corner over there. You'll soon get used to things."

They heard raised voices coming from the office next door. The super was arguing with DI Frank Carlisle. Seconds later, he stuck his head around the adjoining door.

"A car's been dragged out of the canal by the visitor centre. A couple of lads saw it bobbing about in the water and they reckon they saw someone in the passenger seat. Go take a look, Matt. Find out what's going on."

"We're up to our eyes in the Potter murder, sir," Matt said. From the raised voices, it was obvious to Matt that Carlisle had argued the toss, and the short straw was now being handed to him.

"What'll it take? An hour tops out of your precious time. Take DS Baxter with you and report back to me." Talbot turned to Kate, and Matt watched the super's eyes run over her slender frame. "You'll do fine with us, lass. You've done the right thing coming here. This side of them hills is a far better place to be. Give it a few weeks and you'll see."

Talbot left, still smiling.

Matt shook his head. "Still fighting the wars of the roses, that one. Take no notice. He means well enough."

"What d'you reckon to the car then? Dumped?" Lily asked.

"Let's hope so. Anything more serious and the boss will have to give it to Carlisle. We have the Potter killing on our plates. Find out what you can about the man, Lily. Speak to other shopkeepers around the High Street. He both lived and worked there. Surely he must have been friendly with someone."

He and Kate made their way down to the car park.

"Are we any further with finding a motive, sir?" Kate said. "Do you have any theories as to why Potter was killed?"

"It wasn't robbery. He wasn't a wealthy man, so there was no money to speak of. According to everyone who knew him, he was just an ordinary bloke. A bit sharp at times according to his secretary, but that's no motive for murder."

"In that case we're looking for secrets," Kate said decisively. "Something Potter knew. Something his killer didn't want to become common knowledge."

That was one line of enquiry, but they'd need to know a lot more about how Potter lived his life and who he spent time with.

"That wife of his," she suggested. "There's a huge gap in their ages. Perhaps we should look a little closer at her."

"And we will. Let's get this little detour over with first."

"Do you know this visitor centre?" Kate asked.

"Yes. It's where the canal reappears after going under the Pennines. From Diggle to Marsden, it runs completely underground."

Kate shuddered. "Working the boats back then must have been grim."

By the time they arrived, the car park was filling up. A uniform was trying to keep order but the press was already on it. They all clamoured for answers, but they would have to wait. The car was in the process of being hauled out of the water. The driver's door was hanging open, with water pouring out of it. Several windows were smashed and the front bodywork was crumpled. Minutes later, the vehicle was dumped on the bank.

Matt and Kate moved forward. Matt shouted for the uniformed officers to keep the crowds back. The boys had been right. Still belted into the passenger seat was the badly burned body of a man.

"This is weird," Kate said. "The car isn't burned at all, just him. It looks like he met his end, was strapped into the car and dumped here."

"What chance of an identity, I wonder?" Matt was frowning at the charred corpse.

"We need a pathologist," Kate shouted to a uniformed officer. "And get CSI up here as quickly as possible."

"We didn't put the call out before," the officer explained. "Some story told by two lads . . . they could have been having a joke."

"Well, this is no joke." Matt's voice was grim. "The poor man has been brutally murdered."

"Think whoever did it wanted him found, sir?" Kate asked.

"The canal is relatively shallow here, so yes, I do."

* * *

It took an over an hour for Doctor Bibby and a CSI team to arrive. "From the looks of the corpse it won't be easy, Matt. You'll have to give me time on this one. Will it be you taking the case?"

"I don't know, Sid. I'm knee deep in another murder at the moment, the Ronald Potter killing."

Bibby nodded. "I'll do an interim report and send it to Talbot."

"I'll tell him."

"Back to the station?" Kate asked.

"We'll bring the super up to speed. With any luck he'll assign Carlisle's team to this one."

"I wouldn't mind a look at that property on Westgate. It was the Potter murder scene. I should familiarise myself with it."

She had a point. "Alright. The station first, then on to Westgate."

They had just arrived back when the desk sergeant called out to Matt.

"DI Brindle, a woman came in earlier, someone called Christine Fletcher. Her daughter, Karen Fletcher, or Kaz as she's known, is missing. She's been gone three days and nights now."

"How old?" Matt asked.

"Sixteen. Her mother reckons something must be up. She has a six-week-old infant and this isn't like her. She's not made contact at all."

"Did the girl leave of her own accord?" Matt asked.

"Her mum said so. She's looked in all the usual places, but no luck."

"Do you have a description?"

"She left a photo."

"Get it circulated and tell uniform to keep a look out."

"Runaways," she said. "Load of hassle. It's not worth the bother, believe me. I have a younger brother who's tried that one often enough, but he always ends up coming home."

"He lives with you?" Matt asked.

"Yes, so he's had to endure the move too. He's not happy. He misses his mates. Zane's only nineteen. It's been difficult for him."

Talbot Dyson was in the incident room looking at the board for the Potter case. "How was it?"

"Definitely murder," Matt told him. "Sid will let us know what his initial findings are as soon as. As yet we don't even have a motive, Talbot. We're still sifting through the man's life and known associates."

"Okay, keep me posted."

Matt threw Kate the car keys. "You drive, my leg is giving me jip." He rubbed at his right thigh. "I went for a run yesterday, thought I might get back into training. Bad idea."

"I don't mean to be personal or anything, but I did notice you have a limp. Old injury?" Kate asked.

"Yes. A year ago, I was nearly blown up. My leg was ruined. I'm trying hard to get back to full fitness, hence the running. But it's a struggle." He frowned. "But the worst part was that I wasn't alone when it happened. If I'm honest, the memories hurt more than the wounds these days. Particularly when I think of my old partner, Paula. DS Wright was killed in the same incident. I was the lucky one. At least I lived to tell the tale."

Talking about Paula Wright, who'd been his sergeant, always upset him. Worse still, if he'd had his wits about him, it would never have happened. Following a tip-off about a meet between drug dealers, the two of them had gone to a lonely spot up on the moors without backup. He should have taken more care, been suspicious. A tip-off just when one was needed, and from an untried source. The thought of his own stupidity made him feel sick, especially because it was Paula who'd paid the price.

They'd been searching an old abandoned building when they'd been hit — a hand grenade thrown through a broken window, and no time to react. Paula was killed outright, and Matt sustained serious injuries. During the long months of recovery, he was certain that he'd never work in CID again. He had difficulty living with himself. Working in the surroundings he'd shared with Paula would kill him, he was sure. But he'd been wrong. He was back, and despite his doubts, settling nicely.

Chapter 6

The house on Westgate no longer looked so appealing. In the last couple of days, it had gained itself a gruesome reputation. Matt and Kate pulled up outside and regarded the property.

"An ordinary enough house," he said.

"From what I've read on the incident board, and heard, our victim was an ordinary man," Kate said. "So far we have nothing that makes Potter a potential murder victim."

"He upset someone, and it happened here," Matt said. "We should ask ourselves who knew where he would be that afternoon."

She shrugged. "Any number of people. The office, the client — and she could have told folk. Why keep it a secret? He could have been followed, of course."

"The client, Dawn Benson." Matt checked his notebook. "The sale was going through. Her statement said she wanted to show her sister around the place."

"Nothing wrong with that," Kate said. "Buying a house is a big deal. I should know, I'm going through the process myself. The house I'm in at the moment is rented.

She wanted a second opinion, that's all. Shame she's had to pull out. Not that I blame her. Who'd want to live in a house where someone has just been murdered?"

Matt gave Kate a quizzical look. Had she inadvertently hit on something? "What are you getting at?" he said.

Kate shook her head. "If it wasn't about Potter — if Potter hadn't seriously upset someone, what *was* it about? If not him, then we have to consider something else, like this house."

"It's an ordinary semi, on your average road." Matt took the estate agent's pamphlet from his file and flipped through it.

A uniformed officer had been posted to keep people out. He recognised Matt, and nodded. Scenes of crime officers were still finishing off, so the front door was open and they went in.

One of the CSIs came forward. "I need a word, sir. We've found something outside." He led the way to the front of the house.

Matt looked around. At first glimpse, everything looked perfectly normal. Then he spotted it. "What's that?" He pointed to a rectangular metal grid on the ground under the front window.

"The coalhole," Kate said. "You must have seen them before. The houses on this street have been here seventy years or more. Back in the day when we all used coal, the coalman delivered and tipped a sackful down here. It went straight into the cellar, so no need to cart mucky coal through the house."

"This house doesn't have a cellar. At least it isn't listed in here." He passed her the estate agent's pamphlet.

"Perhaps they forgot. That grill has been sealed for years. Put a couple of plant pots over it, and you'd never know it was there."

"We're about to start a search for the cellar door, sir," the CSI said. "There must be a way down to the cellar from inside the house. Otherwise how did they get at the coal?" He gave Kate a smile.

"The kitchen or the hallway is the usual place." Kate led the way back inside.

Another CSI was waiting for them inside. "The kitchen is clear now, sir. We've taken swabs from all the surfaces. Results'll be in asap."

"Did you find anything obvious?" Matt asked.

"Apart from all the blood, you mean? There was a trace of something on the door of that unit," he pointed to one of the wall units, "as if something brushed along it. We'll let you know what we find."

"Even if we do come across a cellar, there's no guarantee it'll help," Matt said.

"Perhaps there's something stashed in there. The proceeds of a crime, something like that?"

The CSIs were moving anything not fastened down away from the kitchen wall. A floor to ceiling fridge-freezer stood in one corner. "What do you think?" Kate said.

Matt and one of the CSIs started to ease it away from the wall. A gap of a few centimetres allowed him to look behind it. There it was, the cellar door. Soon, the fridge was in the centre of the kitchen and the door exposed. It had been sealed shut with wooden planks nailed across it. Matt went to take a closer look. The wood was new, as were the nails. This had been done recently. The crime scene investigators got to work. The job took a while — whoever had sealed the door didn't intend anyone to go down there again.

Finally, the senior CSI pulled on it and it creaked, groaned and scraped against the kitchen floor. The staircase leading down was filthy with the dust of years, but in the centre of each step it was just possible to make out faint footprints.

Kate flicked through the pamphlet again. "I bet the agents didn't even know it was here."

Matt pointed to the footprints. "Someone has been down here recently. Come on, let's take a look." One of the CSI officers handed him a torch, and Matt led the way down.

The cellar consisted of one room. There were no lights, and black coal dust coated most of the floor and the uneven roughly plastered walls.

Matt shone the torchlight into every corner, while Kate watched intently. "There's nothing here," she said.

Matt moved a little further in. There was a faint chink of daylight coming from one edge of the metal cover of the old coal hole. He squinted at the floor beneath it. Kate was wrong, there was something. He could just make out several blackened shapes lying on the floor. He gingerly nudged one with his foot. Whatever it was moved slightly. He knelt down and pointed the torchlight directly onto them. He could scarcely believe his eyes. The sight was grotesque.

"Get one of the crime scene bods down here," he ordered Kate.

"Found something, sir?"

Matt turned to her, grim faced. "If I'm not mistaken, these are bones lying here. They look human to me."

* * *

"What are you suggesting, lad? That Potter was done in to cover up an old murder?"

"It's one theory. Given what we've found, we have to weigh up everything. But it's more likely that Potter stumbled upon something."

"What sort of something? Any ideas?"

"No. We've a long way to go yet. But we have to consider that someone didn't want that house messing with because they knew those remains would be discovered. Once it becomes a murder scene, the current buyer drops out and the house loses its appeal. Given the way rumours circulate, it could well sit on the market for ages before the owner tries to sell it again. But it's a gamble. They must realise that being a murder scene, forensics would go over every inch of the place."

Talbot Dyson looked doubtful. "Whether it was about the house or something Potter found out, or even Potter himself, we still need a motive."

"And that's the hard part. He was just an ordinary bloke, neither particularly liked nor disliked. He just got on with his life and his job. As yet, we can find no enemies. There was no robbery. He does have money, but most of that is earmarked for his son. The rest is tied up in the house she and his son live in. In short, there is no reason why Potter should be a murder victim. Then again, the woman who was set to buy made no secret of her plans for the house. The front extension alone would have uncovered the cellar. Perhaps the killer was desperate. One way or another, the transaction had to be stopped."

"That's a bit of a leap. You think whoever is responsible for that body did for Potter too?" Talbot said.

"We have no way of knowing that yet. We'll have to dig a bit to get at the truth."

"And get some evidence. Don't forget that," Talbot added.

"We'll see what Doctor Bibby can do for us. But I want that house searched, top to bottom." Matt paused. Talbot wasn't going to like the next bit. It would be costly and mean tying up staff. "Some digging will be required too. The garden, both back and front. From what I saw, that was not a complete skeleton we retrieved."

Talbot Dyson shook his head. "Bloody hell! Can we see what Sid has to say first?"

"Someone was murdered in that house before Potter. Perhaps more than one, we have no way of knowing. We need to do that search, sir."

"Okay. Do what you have to, but keep me posted. I'd give you a hand, but I'm working on that other case with

Carlisle." Talbot Dyson was still frowning when Matt left the office.

"What now?" Lily asked.

"I'd like to know more about the buyer, Dawn Benson. We also need a list of tenants."

"I can get on with that one. Going back how long?"

"No idea. That depends on what the good doctor can tell us about the age of those bones."

"Incidentally, I can't find anything incriminating about Potter, Francine or Mary Salter. They have no record between them, not even a parking ticket."

Chapter 7

A bright light shone directly onto her face, and she heard a noise like cutlery being washed. She lay on her back, covered to her neck in a sheet. Her head hurt. More drugs? She turned her head to one side. What she saw made her scream. Next to her was a small table on which stood a bowlful of bloody water, and lying beside it, a scalpel and a pair of pliers.

"What have you done to me?"

"Nothing much. You didn't feel anything, I made sure of that. Complain, and next time I won't be so considerate."

"What do you want?"

"Tell me about Caroline. Where she's hiding will do for starters."

The girl was confused. "I don't know any Caroline."

"Yes, you do. The pair of you were friends. You worked together in that place. You must remember her. She was pretty, with long dark hair and she always had that red handbag with her."

"What place? I've no idea what you're on about. You've got it wrong, got me mixed up with someone else.

I'm telling you the truth. I don't know Caroline, so I can't help you."

The girl felt a sudden sharp pain in her right hand. She screamed, and got a slap across the face for her trouble.

"I don't have much patience. I need the truth. I have time and effort invested in this. You will speak to me or I'll get rid. You know what that means, don't you? No more of your lies. I have photographs of you and Caroline laughing together. You do know her, so talk to me."

The girl's hand was aching like hell. She was still in the same small, damp room, tethered to the wall by the chain. She couldn't sit up and she couldn't raise her arm. She'd no idea what had been done to her.

A woman stood over her, masked and gowned like a surgeon.

"Help me or suffer the consequences. See?" Her captor held up a pair of large tweezers. Gripped between them was a bloodied fingernail. "So far you're lucky. You're only missing two, one each from your little fingers. It's up to you. Tell me where Caroline is and I'll stop. Refuse, and you'll suffer the consequences. I'll rip off the others without anaesthetic."

The girl was horrified. Seeing the nightmarish evidence of what had been done to her made her fingers suddenly begin to throb. She cried out in shock and pain.

"I won't stop at fingernails either. I have a whole range of medical instruments. Don't tempt me to practise my blossoming skills any further."

"You can't!" she shrieked. "This is insane. I promise you, I know nothing about any Caroline."

The woman had hold of her left hand. "Pity. What elegant fingers you have. Do you imagine for a moment that if things were reversed, she'd protect you? The person who's paying me is ruthless. Tell me where Caroline is hiding and I'll let you keep these intact. Refuse, and I'll take your nails and then the tips of each finger. The stumps will bleed. In this filth, they'll likely become infected. Then you'll be ill. Not a nice way to go, is it? But it's up to you. Tell me what I want to know, or die alone, cold and in agony."

Shock and confusion deprived her of speech. Her head felt fuzzy. Seconds later, she passed out.

* * *

"Tomorrow I want all the residents on Westgate interviewed. Someone might have seen or heard something, even if they didn't realise it was important. If any of them have CCTV, we need that too."

"Want me to do that, sir?" Lily asked Matt.

"Did you have any luck with the shopkeepers along Marsden High Street?"

"Nothing new. Potter kept himself to himself. He opened on time, did okay trade, and that's about it."

Matt checked the time. "Go to Westgate first thing in the morning. Take a couple of uniforms with you. In the meantime, there's the list of tenants to sort through. Kate will help you with that one. I'll speak to this Julie, the part-timer at the agency."

Talbot Dyson came into the office. "We still have that missing girl, Karen Fletcher. Her mother was in here earlier. Given that we've got a pile of bones, I thought we should keep it in mind. Particularly as a trainer was found in the layby on the Sheffield Road in New Mill. We could do with ruling it out. Check that hostel in Huddersfield too. Her mother thinks she could have stayed there."

Matt frowned. "The trainer might be significant, or it might not. Once I've spoken to Doctor Bibby, we'll have a better idea. But the chances are, sir, that she's just run away. She has a history apparently."

"I've got a bad feeling," Talbot said. "Instinct, lad, never let me down yet. Besides, Christine Fletcher, the mother, is likely to run to the press at the drop of hat.

She'll accuse us of all sorts. If you've got the time, pop along and have a word."

"Can't Carlisle's team take up some of the slack?"

"He's got a lot on with that car in the canal."

Had Matt not been knee deep in the Potter case, he would have liked to pursue that one. He'd been there when the car was pulled out, and seen the state of the body. He was curious, so when Talbot had left he said to Lily, "Have a chat with Beckwith, see what you can find out about that."

"I think they may be close to getting an ID," she said. "Beckwith was looking at some old records earlier, requesting stuff from Leeds. I'll see him later in the pub. I'll be in there with Greg, my fella. Get a couple of pints down Beckwith, and he'll loosen up."

"I'll nip into Pennine Forensics on my way in tomorrow. I want to see what they're making of the bones we found in that cellar," Matt said.

"That's most likely an old case too. Once they've been confirmed as definitely human, Dyson will have us looking through the old mispers records," Lily said.

Chapter 8

Day 3

Evelyn Brindle stared out of the French windows across the lawn that swept down to the lake. "Those fairground people are setting up today. It's only six thirty and already there is an HGV rolling across the bottom field. I hope they don't do any damage."

"It's only for three days, Ma," Matt said.

"Damage or not, there'll be litter everywhere, and we'll both see and hear them from the house. I hope there's not too much noise, Matthew."

"We have no neighbours to disturb, so it hardly matters."

Evelyn Brindle was a worrier. She'd never reconciled herself to Matt's idea to open up Brindle Hall to the public. The thought of having strangers wandering around the estate was anathema to her. Granted, they needed the money, but was all this upheaval and change really necessary? Was there no easier way to get the money?

"Sarah isn't happy with us having the event either," Evelyn said. "She's worried that the staff won't cope.

Suppose there's trouble? At a similar event in Halifax they had youths running riot with knives."

"That was fake news," Matt said. "Some lunatic posted it on the internet trying to stir up trouble. People were quick to take it as gospel, but there was no truth in it. The event in Halifax went off without a hitch."

But Evelyn Brindle remained unconvinced. "We'll have crowds, Matthew. It's your sister who will have to cope, she'll have to organise everything. You won't be here."

"Attracting crowds is the whole idea, Ma. Money, remember? They come once, they'll come again. Bring the kids to the farm, spend money. We'll soon get known."

Evelyn knew she was fighting a losing battle. Her son was adamant that this was the way forward. "This came for you yesterday." She handed him a large envelope.

"It's the information about the music festival I'm thinking of putting on next spring."

"Music festival! Matthew, that is even worse than the debacle going on down there today! People with tents, all the mud, and horrendous noise into the small hours. You have to think again, son. This whole thing has gone far enough."

"Calm down, Ma. I'll speak to Sarah. We'll see how this event goes first and take it from there."

* * *

"As you can see from the state of the bones, burning was incomplete. The leg bone still has flesh attached, though it's dry and fragile and gone like leather in parts." Sid Bibby touched the bone with a gloved hand and a fragment of blackened skin fell off. "We don't have a complete body either. We have the left femur, arm bones, part of the ribcage and the pelvis. That is useful. I can tell you straight away that the victim is female."

"No head?" Matt asked.

Sid pursed his lips. "They're still looking. It would help with identification. There are no hands or feet either."

"Any idea how old she was, or how long she'd been in that cellar?"

"Give me a chance, Matt. A few days and I should have more information for you. But I can tell you this. She was dismembered first. See?" He pointed. "The neck of the femur is still attached, but there is evidence of it having been sawn through. Given that, I'd say the body parts were burned individually."

"In that case, there is every possibility that there are other body parts somewhere in that house."

"I'll leave that one with you, but it's going to be well-nigh impossible to identify her from what we have here."

"I've read somewhere that it's possible to get DNA from marrow in the long bones, particularly the femur," Matt said.

"It's been badly burned, Matt. I'll do tests, but even then it may not be possible. I'll let you know."

Dismembered and burned added up to murder. That was two victims the house on Westgate had claimed. But why? Were they linked?

"How are you doing with the body in the car?" Matt asked. "That one was burnt to a crisp too."

"That's Carlisle's case," Sid reminded him. "But we are faring a little better with that one, despite the damage."

"You have an ID?"

"Carlisle already has the name, so there's no harm in telling you. It appears the body is that of Paul Ainley."

Paul Ainley was a criminal who had managed to evade justice for most of his nefarious career. He was local and well known, but as far as Matt was aware, he'd been quiet recently.

"Wonder who he upset?"

"It wasn't pleasant," Sid said. "He was clobbered about the head, knocked unconscious and then set alight. Whoever did it was keen to hide his identity."

"What swung it then? The ID? It must be as impossible to get DNA from that body as it is from this one, surely."

"He was still wearing his watch. It had an inscription on the back. Plus, evidence of old arm and rib fractures he got skiing a couple of years ago."

"Is that enough?" Matt asked.

"Carlisle spoke to the family and he seems to think so. If he does want DNA evidence, it'll take a while and be costly. Ask Talbot. He'll fill you in."

* * *

Matt got back into his car and rang Lily. She was with a uniformed constable in Westgate, knocking on the neighbours' doors. So far, she'd not met with much luck.

"I'm going to the estate agents," he told her. "I want an address for the part-timer, Julie. A quick word, and then back to the station. We'll meet later and collate what we've got."

The way things were going, it wouldn't be much. It wasn't easy to piece together Ronald Potter's life. The man did absolutely nothing that made him unusual. He was only known in the community because of his job, selling houses. As for the rest of it, he kept himself to himself.

What's Kate up to?" Matt asked.

"She's investigating the previous tenants of the house, sir."

"Let's hope she turns up something useful."

Matt was parking up when his mobile rang. It was Talbot.

"Have a word with Christine Fletcher urgently, will you? She's doing the desk sergeant's head in with her constant phone calls. All she needs is a couple of words of comfort. Tell her we're doing what we can. We've picked up the trainer. She's confirmed that it's not her daughter's. We have no reason to believe Karen has met with any harm. If the girl hasn't come home by the end of the week, we'll put out an appeal in the press. That should calm the woman down."

Matt groaned. "I'm working on a case, sir. There have been two murders at that house on Westgate. Doctor Bibby confirmed the second one when he examined the bones I found. It's a tricky one. I'm pushed for resources as it is."

"I've given you an extra body. DS Baxter is a good copper. Came highly recommended. Get Christine Fletcher sorted, and I'll organise the search of the house. No choice now, 'ave I?"

At least that was something. Matt decided to speak to Mary Salter about Julie first and then go to New Mill to see the Fletcher woman.

* * *

"You're in luck," Mary Salter said. "She'll be back in a minute. She's gone to the shop to get some coffee."

"What are her hours?" he asked.

"It varies. If we're busy, then I give her a ring. Julie is a part-time student, you see. Today she's helping me shift the backlog of paperwork. If no one takes over, I expect we'll be closing down soon."

A young woman of about nineteen came in through the office door.

Matt smiled at her. "DI Matt Brindle. I'm investigating Ronald Potter's murder. Do you mind answering some questions?"

The girl shook her head. "Ask away."

"Were you working on the day Mr Potter was killed?"

Matt saw her turn to Mary Salter as if seeking guidance.

"Yes."

"Were you here when Dawn Benson rang the office?"

Another look at Mary Salter. "Er — I'm not sure. I think I might have gone by then."

She was blushing. The girl had lied. "Think again, Julie. You must tell me the truth. Did you answer the phone when Dawn Benson rang?"

"No, I'd defo gone by then," she said. "I had to do some shopping for my mum."

"What do you want her to say, Inspector?" Mary Salter sounded annoyed.

"I'm trying to find out who was in this office and who wasn't," Matt said, irritated now.

Mary Salter rose from her chair and faced him. "You think it was me, don't you? You think I knifed Ronald?"

"All I want is the truth. I have to ask these questions. If you were out and Julie was taking care of the office, then that does give you the opportunity."

"Opportunity my eye! I would never harm Ronald. I worked with the man, for God's sake! We were friends, sometimes a bit more than that." She turned away. "You can't seriously think that I could kill a man so brutally? You're off your head!"

Chapter 9

The Fletchers lived on a social housing estate roughly half a mile from the centre of New Mill. The place had seen better days. The houses had been state of the art when they were built in the fifties. But over half a century later, most of them were still rented and in dire need of refurbishment.

Matt had been told that Christine Fletcher lived with her daughter Karen, a son called Caleb, and the infant. At eighteen, Caleb was older than Karen.

A woman, obviously Christine, opened the door to him. "Have you found her?" she said immediately.

He heard a dog barking inside and looked past the woman to the beast desperately trying to jump over the gate separating the kitchen from the rest of the house.

"He's harmless," Christine Fletcher said.

Matt doubted it. The dog, a pitbull cross, looked damned annoyed about something.

"Come inside. We'll talk in the front room."

The house was untidy, with baby stuff scattered all over the place. A pram stood under the window, and a clothes airer stood in front of the gas fire, which was going full blast. All the chairs had packs of nappies and other infant paraphernalia on them.

"The mess is down to our Kian. He's damned hard work, and I have sole charge of him until his mother decides to return," Christine Fletcher said.

"You're sure you've no idea where Karen has gone?"

She snorted. "Do you think I'd put up with this lot if I had? Kian's a lovely baby, but he never shuts up. I've done with all that. He's Kaz's responsibility, not mine. He's only six weeks old, and not an easy baby."

"Does Karen usually take care of him? She doesn't rely on you?"

"No. I told her straight, the kid is yours and I want no part of it."

Christine's bottom lip trembled. "I've been too hard on her. She's only sixteen. That's no age to be bringing up a kid, is it?"

Matt said nothing to this. "How was Karen before she left?"

"Edgy I suppose. I kept asking her what was wrong but she wouldn't tell me owt. I had the feeling she was in danger."

"What sort of danger? It could have some bearing on what's happened to her."

"I've no idea. Not good at sharing stuff is our Kaz. But she mixed with some weird types."

"Can you give me any names?"

"No. Look, you have to find her. The stupid bitch should never have left the kid. She knows I can't cope. The bloody noise he makes gets me down. I don't sleep, so I lie awake all night worrying about Kaz and what's happened to her."

"Has she done this before?"

Christine nodded.

"And she came back safe?" Another nod. "Then it's highly likely that she's done the same thing this time. She's young, and as you said, being tied down with an infant at sixteen must be very difficult."

"Wasn't thinking about that when she had her knickers round her ankles, was she? I could bloody kill her. Leaving me with all this worry and him to look after." She nodded to the pram.

"Where does she usually go? Are you sure you don't know who any of her friends are?" Matt asked.

"She ran off a year ago. She went to that women's hostel in Huddersfield. The woman that runs it, Pamela Ansel, she rang me. I didn't worry so much then because I knew she was safe. The mob she hangs out with all live round here. If she were with one of them, someone would have told me by now."

"You've checked with the hostel?"

She nodded. "They've not seen her."

"If she isn't back by the weekend, we'll do an appeal. It'll go out on the local TV news and in the paper. Someone will see it. Karen will get the message."

Matt let himself out. Closing the front door behind him, he turned and saw a young woman smiling at him.

"Matt! What are you doing here?"

It was his one-time girlfriend, Melissa, now a social worker with the Huddersfield team.

"The daughter has gone missing," he said. "I could ask you the same question."

"Christine asked me to come. I know this family of old. She isn't doing very well with the infant, and she's asked for help."

"By help you mean she wants you lot to take him into care?"

"You know I can't discuss the Fletcher case, Matt. But I'm hopeful that that isn't going to happen. I'm sure Kaz will see sense and come home soon enough."

Before the incident that damaged him, Matthew had been in love with this woman. During the long months of recovery, he'd ended the relationship, not thinking it fair to saddle Melissa with his problems. Physically, he'd been a wreck. Mentally, he'd been depressed and prone to panic attacks. Melissa held down a tough job. In his opinion, the last thing she needed was him on her back. The problem was, Melissa saw it differently.

"Want to go for a drink sometime?" The words were out before he could stop them.

"Why? Think we might have something to salvage? Or is it just guilt asking?" With that, she barged past him and knocked on the Fletchers' door.

* * *

Westgate might be a pleasant street, but there were at least fifty houses along it. So far, they'd had a response from only four of them.

"The woman who lives next door to the murder is in now," the uniformed officer told Lily. "We could catch her while she's here."

Good idea. If there was anything to be heard that day, she would be the one. Lily knocked on the front door.

It was soon answered. "I'm DC Haines from East Pennine CID," Lily said. "Could I ask you a few questions about next door?"

"About the murder, you mean?" The woman gave Lily a conspiratorial smile. "Yes, love, come inside."

Word had got around. Lily wondered how far down the street the news had reached. She left the uniformed PC outside and followed the woman into the house. Her name was Edna Golding and she lived alone. In the time it took to reach the sitting room, Lily learned that Edna had been widowed for ten years, played bingo and went to the social club in the village once a week.

"It got a bit noisy at one point. I had to bang on the wall with this." She held her walking stick aloft. "We're not used to noise round here. It's a quiet street as a rule, nothing much happens. Well it doesn't now those girls have moved out. But given the murder and all, this street's reputation is shot." She seemed unconcerned at this. "That house will never sell now. I mean, who'd want it? Lying on the kitchen floor in a bloody heap I was told."

Ignoring this, Lily asked. "You heard an argument? When was this?"

"Just after lunchtime. He arrived, that estate agent chap, and a few minutes later, she turned up. They had a right set to. She was screaming at him, swearing an' all. I couldn't get what it was about, but he must have done something to upset her."

"Do you know who the woman was?"

"Her that works with him. I know because I went in their office a few weeks back. My daughter's looking for a place. Right piece of work, she is."

"Are you talking about Mary Salter?"

"Yes, love."

"Did you see her leave?"

"They argued for a good ten minutes, then she sped off in that car of hers, the silver one. The place was as quiet as a grave after that. Never heard another peep. Was it her that did for him?"

"We don't know yet. We are still investigating. You spoke of girls living there. Were they the last tenants?"

"Yes. Out until all hours they were. To start with there was two of them, but I think they moved a mate in after a while. I didn't see much of her. She rarely went out. But the other two, they were out every night, done up to the nines the both of them."

"Do you know their names?"

"No, love. A quick hello across the street, that's all the communication we had."

"You've been very helpful, Mrs Golding. Someone will come round later and take a statement from you."

The woman looked excited. "Gosh. I've never been a witness to anything before. Will I have to go to court?"

"We'll have to wait and see." Lily couldn't help smiling.

Outside in the street, Lily rang Matt. "The next-door neighbour heard Potter and Salter arguing. One heated row later, Salter left. The woman reckons she heard nothing after that."

"Well done. Keep asking. See if you can get some CCTV. A timed shot of Mary Salter's car would be perfect."

"When do we talk to her?" Lily asked.

"I'll go and bring her in. Mary Salter has just become our main suspect."

Chapter 10

Matt rang Pennine Forensics and spoke to the senior man, Doctor Graham Harwood. He wanted to know if they'd managed to identify the residue found on the kitchen cabinet door at the house on Westgate. After speaking to Mary Salter, he had a theory.

"Turns out it was hair lacquer," Graham Harwood said. "We've also found a hair — blonde — and a couple of fingerprints. How hairspray ended up on that wall is something else. It's good news. I'll email you an image of the prints. Get a suspect, and you can try for a match. We are also sifting through ash and rubbish that we found in the cellar. It might yield something."

Now they were getting somewhere. Mary Salter was fond of her cosmetics. If the hair lacquer and prints did belong to her, that put her at the scene. The argument put her there at the right time.

"I think she was sitting on the worktop. She leaned back, and there you are," Matt said.

"Yes, that would work."

"Not only that, but if she was sitting like that she'd be at the right height to inflict the wound." Matt put the phone down and turned to Kate, who was engrossed in her research. "Fancy a break? I'm off to the estate agents to bring Mary Salter in."

Kate managed a faint smile and grabbed her coat from the back of her chair. "That house has had ten tenants during the last six years, all couples or single occupants with jobs. No families. Don't you think that's odd? It is a family home after all."

"Anything known about any of them?" Matt asked.

"Not yet. I'm still working through the list."

"Any of them young women?"

"Doesn't look like it."

* * *

They arrived to find Mary Salter alone in the estate agent's office. She didn't look pleased to see them, especially when Matt asked her to accompany them to the station to answer some more questions.

"Can't we do that here? I've got a load of paperwork to see to. This place is scheduled to close at the end of the week. If I don't do it now, I'm won't have the time."

"Sorry, but this won't wait."

She gave him a filthy look. "I've told you everything I know. What more can you possibly want?"

"We have fresh evidence that puts you at the scene of the crime. You can arrange for your solicitor to meet you there if you wish," Matt said.

Her eyes widened. "Whoever you've got will do. I've nothing to hide."

Mary Salter sat with Kate in the back seat of Matt's car, looking sullen. She said not a word all the way to the police station in Huddersfield.

"I'll arrange for the duty solicitor to come in." Matt handed her over to a uniformed officer who escorted her to an interview room.

"Down to her, was it?" Talbot Dyson had been watching her come in.

"She hasn't told us the truth about the afternoon Ronald Potter was killed, that's for sure. We have forensics that put her at the house. A neighbour heard the two of them arguing and she saw her there as well. I want to know what she was up to, and why she didn't simply tell us the truth in the first place."

"What about the bones?" asked Talbot.

"That's another matter. Doctor Bibby's still working on them. Not as fast as he's working on the other body. Carlisle has an ID already, I believe."

"Yes, we've had a bit of luck on that one. The x-rays showed up the old breaks in the arm and ribs. Ainley's sister confirmed that they had indeed been broken. She recognised the watch too. It was a gift from their parents for his twenty-first."

"What about DNA? You know, to make absolutely sure," Matt asked.

"No chance. Not without weeks of testing anyway. The man was doused in petrol and set alight. Whoever is responsible didn't want anything to remain that would help us identify him."

"So, why? And why did he miss the watch? I wonder how that happened?"

"All that burnt flesh — more than likely it wasn't noticed. Paul Ainley was a villain. He won't be missed."

Matt was still doubtful. "Anything else to help with the identity?"

"There was a woman's red handbag in the boot, empty but unscathed."

"Does it belong to his wife?" Matt asked.

"She says not. It's with forensics now." Talbot changed the subject. "If the Potter killing is down to this woman, and she isn't responsible for those bones, so much for your theory about the house."

He had a point. As far as Matt could discover, there was still no reason to kill Potter. It had to be about the house and what was hidden in that cellar. But what did that have to do with Mary Salter? He took his phone from his pocket and rang Lily.

"Would you go and speak to Dawn Benson? Ask her about the house and who she'd told about the alterations she intended to make. Also, ask about the phone call she made to the office that afternoon. Was it a young person she spoke to, or was it Mary Salter?"

* * *

"You've got it horribly wrong. I could never harm Ronald. I . . . I . . ."

"You what, Miss Salter? Loved him?"

The woman actually blushed. "I didn't say that," she demurred. "I was fond of him though. He could be a bad tempered old bugger, but I'm not getting any younger. Him and me had been good together once. I tried to persuade him to give it another go. I certainly didn't want him falling into the clutches of that money-grabber again."

"Who do you mean?" Matt said.

"Francine, his ex-wife."

"What makes you think there was any danger of that?"

"She'd been harassing him. Ringing him up, asking to meet. Ronald told me that she'd been pestering him. She wanted them to be a family again. She thought it best for the child."

Matt shook his head. He didn't believe a word of it. "She never said any of this to me."

"She wouldn't, would she? Francine is crafty. She'll have had her reasons but they'll have had nothing to do with wanting Ronald."

"You went to the house on Westgate. What happened then?"

"I decided to speak to him there because the office is busy. Julie was in that day, and there are always folk coming in and out. There's no privacy. When I turned up, we argued. I told him I thought he was a fool, falling for

Francine's clever chat. He'd agreed to go round to her house, have some dinner and spend the evening playing with Daniel. Once she got him there, that would have been it. Ronald was a good man, but he couldn't resist a pretty face. Francine could wrap him around her little finger."

"Do you know why Francine wanted him back?"

"Money. Has to be. He wasn't much to look at, and Francine is half his age."

"Who does the company accounts?"

"Smith's. They're on the High Street near us, above the florists."

"Get me a copy of the latest ones. It'll do no harm to take a look."

A uniformed officer interrupted them. He handed Matt a note. Lily had rung the station and wanted to speak to him urgently.

"Excuse me a moment. I won't be long," he told Mary and the solicitor.

He went back to the incident room and rang Lily.

"I've just spoken to a couple two doors down from the house. They recall seeing Mary Salter too, but there was another visitor. Within minutes of Salter arriving, a young woman in a red sports car turned up. She went into the house, stayed about ten minutes and then left. From the description, it sounds like Francine Potter, sir."

That put both women at the scene with Potter. In that case, was Mary Salter telling him the truth? Could it have been Francine that killed Potter?

"There's something else. The next door neighbour told me that the last tenants in that house were two young girls. She thinks a third might have joined them. No names, I'm afraid."

"Thanks, Lily. I'll speak to Salter about them."

"Problem, lad?" Talbot asked.

Matt was standing on the corridor, trying to work out what it all meant. "I've got two women at the crime scene, the ex-wife and the secretary. Potter argued with one about the other. I'm trying to decide which one killed him, if either of them did." Matt rubbed his head. "It doesn't square with what we found in the cellar. I'm convinced that Potter's death has less to do with those women and more to do with that house. Apart from which, having spoken to both the women, I don't see either of them being responsible for his murder. They don't seem capable of it."

"You're interviewing the secretary now?"

Matt nodded.

"Bail her. You have her on opportunity, but what's her motive?"

"She doesn't have one. A sudden flash of jealousy about the ex-wife? But I just don't see Mary Salter pulling out a knife and killing him. If she had, Francine would have found the body on the floor in any case. She'd have raised the alarm."

"Like I said, bail her pending further enquiries. Go and speak to the ex again. See what she has to say for herself."

Matt returned to the interview room. "You are free to go, Ms Salter. For now. But before you do, the last tenants, the young women. Do you have their names?"

"What young women? You've got that wrong. The last tenant was a single businessman."

"Would you check that, please? We have information to the contrary. And let me know the name of that last tenant."

Chapter 11

Kate was at Matt's heels as he made for the incident room. "I was watching the interview. You didn't tell her about the body in the cellar."

"No. Until we have more information, that one is need to know only. We'll go and have another word with Francine, see what she has to say for herself."

Matt let Kate drive again. "You let Salter go. Why?" she asked. "You don't think it's down to her?"

"I don't know what to think. She's mixed up in it somewhere, but nothing we've got at the moment points to her being a killer."

Kate pulled out onto the main road. "I'm finally getting the hang of the area. It's very different from driving around the streets of Manchester. I love the lanes and those hills. It's beautiful round here."

"Pity our crime rate doesn't reflect the area. This part of Huddersfield, the outskirts between the moors and the town, is quite well-heeled. Despite that, crime is rife."

"Where do you live?" she asked him.

"A couple of miles away, near the village of Hepworth."

"My brother mentioned that place yesterday. There's an event, a fair in the grounds of some big country house. He plans to go. The big kid!"

Matt smiled. "Hope he behaves himself. The owner, Lady Evelyn, isn't keen. She's on the lookout for the slightest misdemeanour. Anyone puts a foot wrong, and she'll pounce. She has some clout too. The woman has the super on speed dial."

"You know her?" Kate sounded impressed.

"She's my mother."

Her mouth dropped open, but there was no time to say more. They had arrived at Francine Potter's house.

She stood at the door, scowling. "What now?"

Matt smiled at her. "We have a few more questions."

"Make it snappy, I've got a kid to feed."

They were outside on the front step, not the ideal place to conduct an interview. "Can we come in?" Kate asked. "I'm sure you don't want the entire neighbourhood knowing your business."

Reluctantly, Francine led the way inside.

"You said nothing about being at the house on Westgate the afternoon Ronald was killed."

Francine stared at Matt. "Who told you?"

"Your car was seen by a neighbour," he said. "It is rather distinctive."

She folded her arms and looked away. "I wanted a word. Nothing wrong with that."

"What did you talk about?" asked Kate.

"None of your bloody business!"

"I'm afraid it is," Matt said. "He's been murdered, remember that."

"I was going to ask him to come here for his tea, but that woman from his office was in there with him, so I didn't bother."

"But you did see him?" Kate asked.

"The front door was open. I went inside and shouted for Ronald but there was no answer. They were too busy arguing. So I left them to it."

"You didn't go into any of the rooms, have a look around?" Kate asked.

Francine shrugged. "No, why would I?"

"Did you see Mary Salter's car?"

"No idea. I wasn't looking for it."

"Did you go into the kitchen, Francine?" Kate asked.

"No, just the hallway. When I heard the raised voices, I went straight out. I didn't fancy getting involved."

"Are you sure it was Mary Salter Ronald was arguing with?"

"Oh, yes. Loud mouthed, interfering old bat!"

"I take it you don't like her," Matt said.

"It's her who doesn't like me. She's always whispering in Ronald's ear, saying God knows what."

Francine sounded plausible but she couldn't seem to look him in the face. Was she lying? If so, what was she trying to hide? "Now, why do I not believe you?" Matt said. "I think you did see Ronald, and I think you spoke to him. Was that why Mary Salter left? She was seen by a neighbour. They saw you, too. The truth, Francine. Lie, and you'll be charged with withholding evidence."

She scowled at him. "I'm telling the truth. I didn't see him."

"Given that you did go into the house, we'll need a sample of your DNA and your fingerprints. I'll get it arranged," Matt said.

"I've done nothing wrong."

"I want them for elimination purposes. You went inside that house. Might I remind you once again that we're looking for a killer?" He and Kate walked away, leaving Francine watching them from the front step.

"Do you believe her?" asked Kate as they drove back to the station.

"No. I've no idea what happened. The neighbour didn't hear any more voices after Mary Salter left. Whatever was said between him and Francine was said quietly."

* * *

Lily was still out speaking to the residents of Westgate. Matt updated the incident board, and then turned to Kate. "Take another look at that list of tenants. Lily reported that the last were a couple of young girls. Mary Salter denied this, said it was a single man. That's suspicious. Find out who they were. If necessary, we'll have to interview everyone who lived in that house during the last few years. Also, get onto Potter's bank. We could do with a look at his transactions over the last few months. Organise a warrant, will you?"

"DI Brindle!" Talbot Dyson's voice boomed out from his office. "A word."

From the sound of it, the super was not in a good mood. Matt went to see what he wanted.

"They've found more body parts at that house," Talbot said, "buried in the garden under a fruit tree. This time they were in two plastic carrier bags. One contained hands and feet and the other, a head. The hands were too burned to get any prints."

"Gruesome. The head — will we get an identity?"

"Unlikely. Battered to a pulp and burnt, Sid reckons. Everything has gone to the morgue. Sid has asked if you'll go down there."

Matt couldn't understand why the super looked so irritated by this. In a way it was good news. It meant Doctor Bibby had more to work with. Despite the state of the head, its discovery made the chance of getting an identity so much better. "Why the long face, sir?"

"Because this is costing a bloody packet." Talbot gave a humourless laugh. "But we'll have to carry on now. No choice, have we? That house is turning out to be a right problem. We've now got two murders attached to it. Despite your theory, there's still no proof that they're connected. I'm concerned that you'll be short-handed."

Matt smiled. Not like the super to worry about such a detail. But Talbot was right, they would be pushed. "You could give me Beckwith," he suggested.

Talbot shook his head. "He's working with Carlisle. They're up to their necks in it as it is."

"The Paul Ainley murder?"

"He was a bad lot but there's nothing, not so much as a whisper on the street. He knew the pecking order. From what we know, he hadn't upset anyone. So why was he killed?"

"Sounds a lot like our bloke. Ah well, no one going spare, sir, so my little group of oddballs will just have to carry on."

"What d'you mean by that?" Talbot was frowning.

"It occurred to me that you might be lumping us all together — those of us that don't fit elsewhere. Me with my leg, and other issues. Lily, the youngest officer in this nick, who the other teams are reluctant to take on because of her youth. And now you give me DS Baxter, complete with a shed load of attitude."

The super paced the office floor with his hands in his trouser pockets. "Lad, I'm sorry if that's how you see it, but you're wrong. Lily needs moulding. She has the makings of a first class detective. As for t'other one — feisty piece, is she? That should make for an interesting night or two in the pub."

Matt Brindle shook his head in despair. The man was a dinosaur.

"How's it going up at the house? Your mother okay with it now?"

"The event only got going this morning. She'll be gritting her teeth and watching closely."

"I was thinking of having a wander up later this week, maybe take her out for a bit of dinner."

"Ring her first," Matt said.

"Aye, I'll do that."

Matt left the office. He needed to tell the team about the new development. This case had started out simple enough but it was rapidly becoming complicated. The lack of apparent motive caused Matt to seriously consider that Potter had been murdered in order to prevent anyone finding the body hidden in that property.

"The search team have found more body parts," he announced to the others."

Lily gave a low whistle, which earned her a tutting from Kate.

"I'll go to the morgue in the morning," Matt said, "on my way in. I'm hoping that Doctor Bibby can give us something, otherwise we're clutching at straws. Kate, continue looking at the past tenants, those young girls in particular. Speak to Mary Salter again. Make her go through the records. She must know who they are. Anything you think odd, anyone on that list who is known to us, we'll go and see them first. Someone who'd lived in that house didn't want Dawn Benson making alterations. Did you speak to her, Lily?"

"I rang her. She was planning an extension to the front and another one to the back. The cellar would have been found for sure."

"Did she tell you who else knew?"

"She had approached the planning department, and spoken to the neighbours. It wasn't a secret."

"There we are then. That's our answer. With Potter's killing hanging over it, the house is saved. Our killer must have expected the sale to fold, and the place to lie empty for a while longer."

"Shame they didn't realise that it was lack of motive that alerted us to what was really going on. That's what made us get nosey. Now we know the truth, the killer will be worried," Lily said.

"The house has a uniformed presence at all times. Anyone who shows anything but a passing interest in what's going on, we'll be told."

Matt saw Kate checking her watch. Irritating, but it *was* getting late. "We'll call it a day. See you all in the morning."

Before Matt had a chance to say anything else, Kate grabbed her stuff and was gone.

Lily sniffed. "Not so much as a goodbye. Can't make up my mind about her."

Matt threw her a look. He wasn't going be drawn into gossip about other members of the team.

"Sorry, sir. It's just, well, you must have noticed. She isn't very friendly, is she? I presume it's down to that attitude of hers that she got the black eye."

"An argument with a door is what she told me," he said. "Give her time. I'm sure she'll be fine."

Chapter 12

Earlier in the afternoon, Kate had received a text from her mother's care home. Gloria Baxter was acting up again. Kate had said nothing to Brindle or Lily. It was her business, not theirs.

Kate's mother hadn't made the move with her and Zane. It was less stressful for her to remain in familiar surroundings. Good for Gloria, but it meant that whenever Kate wanted to see her, she had to make the tedious journey back to Manchester.

At this time of day, the motorway was busy. The M62 snaked its way through the Pennines, rising and falling with the terrain. At one point, it boasted the highest junction on any UK motorway. The traffic tended to slow down here as it climbed. From the top, Kate could see the queues building up below as the vehicles neared the larger towns surrounding Manchester. It was two hours before she was finally talking to the care home manager.

"What happened? Is she alright?"

The manager smiled. "Gloria is fine, none the worse for her adventure. She was found wandering round the Arndale Centre in town. She drew attention because she was wearing a coat over her nightclothes and asking people for money. The police picked her up and brought her back. Fortunately, she had our card in her coat pocket."

This made Kate angry. "How in the world does something like that happen? And there's nothing fortunate about it. She could have had an accident or been mugged. A vulnerable woman goes walkabout, and is gone long enough to reach the Arndale! Did no one notice?"

"Central Manchester isn't far from here, a mere five minutes on the bus. And Gloria didn't just walk out without us noticing." The manager sounded put out. "Your brother took her. He was here at lunchtime, and said he'd take her for a walk."

"Zane? What the hell was he playing at? I told you that my mother was not to be allowed out with anyone if I wasn't present. Zane is an idiot. He can't even look after himself." Kate inhaled. She was losing it and needed to calm down. Right now, she could have cheerfully throttled her brother. "Can I see her?"

"Gloria is sleeping, but you can stick your head around the door if you want, satisfy yourself that she is fine. Gloria wasn't happy when she got back. She was argumentative and wouldn't settle. We gave her a sedative and then contacted you."

"No matter what he tells you, don't let Zane take her out again. He might be her son, but he's barely able to take responsibility for himself."

After checking on her mother, who was snoring happily, Kate made for home. This wasn't going to work. If she intended to stay with East Pennine CID on a permanent basis, then she'd have to find somewhere nearby for her mother. She couldn't make this journey every time the home called.

The return journey was easier, the motorway traffic had eased. As soon as she got home, she shouted for Zane. Kate knew he was in, she could hear his music blaring out from upstairs.

He came bounding into the sitting room, a big grin on his face and a friend in tow. Their mother could be lying injured somewhere! He obviously didn't give a damn.

"Hi, sis, what's to eat?"

"Get your own!" Her fury of earlier was back. "What the hell did you think you were doing today? Why take her out? And why didn't you raise the alarm when you lost her?"

He backed off, hands up. "Whoa! I thought Mum would like a turn round the shops. I was going to buy her some lunch. But Caleb here developed a dodgy belly. While I was in the bogs seeing to him, Mum did one."

Kate saw the sheepish grin on the lad's face. "Caleb? Sorry, love, entertainment's over, so do one." She shoved him toward the door.

"We'll pick things up tomoz, mate," Zane called after him.

"You have no idea, do you? Our mother is *ill*, Zane. She doesn't do stuff on her own. She could have been attacked, wandered off and fallen in the canal, anything."

"But she didn't. She was fine. We came out of the bogs and the coppers had her in tow. I thought it best to leave them to it. They'd get her back to the home, job done."

"You're a mess, do you know that?"

"I was going for a pint."

"You are going nowhere. You need to rein it in, Zane, or we'll fall out big style."

He shrugged. "Okay, no worries."

Kate took a deep breath. He was right, there was no harm done. She needed to calm down. "A pint? Weren't you planning a visit to that fair out Hepworth way?"

"Changed our minds. Heard a whisper that there's going to be trouble. Best out of it."

Kate made a mental note to tell Matt. "You are grounded for the foreseeable. Understand?"

"Not enough that you embarrassed me in front of a new mate? Not just me that needs to rein it in, sis. You need to watch that temper of yours."

"And you've got a lot to learn."

* * *

Matt's mother paced up and down the main hall. Her agitation was getting on his nerves. So, the fair was noisy. It was to be expected. It was just the sound of youngsters screaming with excitement. The music from the rides was overpowering and the lower field was lit up like a beacon, its lights flashing in the night sky.

"Go and take a look, Matt. Find out when they're packing up. There is no way I can go to bed and sleep with all that going on."

"The fair is going down well, Ma," he said. "Sarah confirmed that trade has been brilliant today. Folk are impressed. They've been to the event and a lot of them will return and visit the house and farm. Why don't I take you down there? You can see for yourself what's going on."

She glanced up at the clock on the wall. "At this time of night? Don't be ridiculous."

"We can have a turn on the waltzers if you like." There was a grin on his face. The likelihood of his mother assenting to this was remote indeed.

"Now you're being silly. You get down there yourself. Make sure those fairground people don't stay any longer than you've agreed."

Matt put on his boots and grabbed a torch. Evelyn Brindle was hard work when everything was ticking along as normal. What was going on currently was way out of her comfort zone and she was impossible.

Things were fine. As agreed, the fair was packing up for the night, and the visitors had started drifting away. He was wandering around the rides and stalls when his phone rang.

"Sir, it's DS Baxter. Hope I'm not disturbing you."

"It's okay. How can I help?"

"My brother, Zane, was planning on going to your event this evening but he cried off. He was told that there was going to be trouble. He won't tell me where he got the information."

"Do you believe him?"

"Yes. Since the move, he's gone a bit wild. He's mixing with some dubious types. He could well have heard it from one of them. He's only nineteen. Your event is exactly the sort of thing he'd normally go to."

"I'm down on the field now, as it happens, and everything is as it should be. It's probably nothing. Tell the lad thanks for his concern."

"Okay, sir, see you tomorrow."

Matt didn't know what to make of the call. He didn't doubt that Kate believed what her brother had told her, but Matt didn't know the young man. He'd reserve judgement.

He heard a woman shouting to him. "This is great, a real good night! You've got this place buzzing, just like you wanted."

It was Melissa. She stood smiling at him, hand in hand with some bloke.

"This is Rod. We work together. Thought I'd show him where my ex lives, so he knows what he has to live up to." She grinned, and punched the man's arm.

Matt gave them a half-hearted smile. "Glad you approve."

"You planning more events like this?" she asked.

"Possibly a music festival next spring."

"We'll have to dust down the tent," she told Rod, and pecked his cheek. "Kaz Fletcher is still missing by the way. Making any progress?"

Matt shook his head. "She sounds like the kind of girl who'll turn up when she's good and ready."

"That's what I told her mother. Well, we're off. See you around."

Matt walked slowly back to the house, shoulders down. It had upset him, seeing Melissa with another man. Their breakup was entirely down to him, but still, part of him hoped she would understand why he'd done it. He'd sent her packing not wanting to saddle her with a cripple. Now it was too late. Melissa had moved on. Perhaps it was time for him to do the same.

Chapter 13

Day 4

"The head is too badly burned for identification," Sid Bibby said. "An attempt was made to incinerate the other body parts found in the second bag, but one of the feet wasn't too badly damaged. There's still a deal of flesh attached to the bones, enough to determine who it belonged to, should you acquire any DNA to compare. It's well-nigh impossible to determine when she died, by the way. I would usually estimate from decomposition, but the burning has made that difficult." He turned a big grin on Matt, and raised a finger. "However. Among the rubbish, we found some newspaper. It was probably used to cover the floor. Er . . . there were no toilet facilities. On one of the scraps, we found a date. A daily from a fortnight ago."

"Dead a couple of weeks at least — and female?"

"The bones of the feet are small and there's nail polish on the toes of the less burned one, so I'd say yes. I'll run DNA tests to make sure."

"A young woman?"

"It looks like it."

Matt nodded. It was now more important than ever that he found out the names of the last tenants.

"This was found embedded in the flesh around the ankle of the less burned foot." Sid Bibby showed Matt a silver anklet that was lying in a kidney dish. "Whoever did this may not have noticed, since the flesh will have swollen in the early stages of the burning. Forensics will clean it up and see if there are traces of DNA. The metal looks like silver but it's very fragile. There is a charm hanging off it just there." He pointed to it. "A red high heeled shoe. Forensics will give it the once over."

It was something. Matt took a photo of the anklet with his mobile. He knew what Talbot would want. He'd ask him to show it to Christine Fletcher, to see if it belonged to her missing daughter. He sighed heavily. He hoped it didn't. Christine Fletcher was on a knife edge as it was.

He rang the station and spoke to Lily. "Sid Bibby came up with something, an item of jewellery. I want to show it to Karen Fletcher's mother. I'll be about an hour."

On the way to New Mill, he tried to make sense of what they had so far. A dead estate agent, murdered for no reason they could find. One dead woman. What, if any, was the connection? The only one he could see was the house. Someone out there didn't want it touching. They knew the body was there and didn't want it found. The work was piling up. The unenviable task of identifying the victim and informing the family weighed heavily on his mind. He hoped that the piece of jewellery hadn't belonged to Karen Fletcher.

Christine Fletcher looked tired and drawn. She came to the door holding the tiny infant in her arms. "Have you found her?"

"I want you to look at something," Matt said gently. "Take your time, and tell me if Karen wore anything like it."

He handed her his mobile with the image on the screen.

She gasped. "She came home with something like this. It was part of the costume she'd been given to wear. Said a man had given it to her and that it went with the job. It was in some club. Waiting on tables, I presumed. We argued. The bloody costume was far too skimpy. I didn't want her flaunting herself in some back street dive." She looked up from the screen. "Where did you get it?"

Matt groaned inwardly. What to tell her? "It was found during our investigations." Tell her the truth at this point, and she'd go to pieces. He'd wait until they knew more — it was pointless jumping to conclusions. "What job, Mrs Fletcher?"

"Some dive in town. I wasn't taking much notice. I flew at her when she told me she was looking for work. Who did she think was going to look after this one? Me, I suppose. I said she'd have to wait until she could get Kian into nursery."

"But she took the job anyway?"

"If that belongs to Kaz, then she must have done, but I'd no idea. She went out a lot, I couldn't stop her. She could have been getting up to anything."

"Are you sure you don't know anything more?"

Christine Fletcher shook her head vigorously.

"I'd like to have her room searched. Are you alright with that?"

"Yes. I haven't touched it since she went."

"Good," he said. "I'll get a team round later today."

* * *

It was mid-morning. The fair on the Brindle estate was up and running again. It was a sunny day, and the crowds were flocking in.

Evelyn was still keeping a wary eye on things, but she was beginning to relent. They were turning a healthy profit, so perhaps Matt was right after all. She decided to take a quick stroll around the perimeter of the lower field with the dog to satisfy herself that there was nothing untoward going on, and then come back to the house for mid-morning coffee.

It was the school holidays, so there were plenty of families making the most of the good weather. They all seemed to be having a good time. It would appear that this was the right way to go. She must learn to trust Matt, stop being so critical of every idea of his. She smiled to herself. He was doing well. Back working at the job he loved, and now running the business. It could all have been so very different. For a while after the incident, Evelyn thought she'd never get the old Matt back.

She was almost at the house when she heard a piercing scream. At first, Evelyn thought it came from the excited children at the fairground. But the second one was even louder. It definitely came from the house, and it sounded like Ivy, the part-time housekeeper. Evelyn's stomach did a somersault. Something was very wrong.

She hurried back and rushed into the main hall. There she saw Ivy, backed into the far corner. Two teenage lads were standing in the middle of the huge room. One of them was clutching a Moorcroft vase that he must have taken from one of the cabinets. Her dog, a small poodle, barked furiously.

"Put that down!" Evelyn ordered, pulling the dog back. "It's very rare and worth a fortune. Drop it, and it can never be replaced."

The lads looked at each other and laughed. The one with the vase held it aloft. "How much will you pay me?"

He was no more than eighteen, and scruffy. The expression on his young face said it all. He wanted an argument. Evelyn was about to remonstrate with him when she spotted the wicked looking knife his friend was clutching.

The second lad lunged at the poodle. "Keep the mutt quiet, or I'll slit its throat."

The lad with the vase held it up again. "C'mon, lady, how much will you give me for the pot? Hurry up, or it won't just be this one. I'll smash the bloody lot."

"You won't get away with it. We have CCTV. You'll be caught and punished." Evelyn eyed the fake camera in the corner of the room. Now she wished she'd done as Matt wanted, and had it installed for real. "You don't seriously want a police record, do you?"

He laughed. "That boat has long since sailed. Cash, or the lot hits the floor. My friends are on the fairground. When they've finished, no one will ever come to this boring old hole again. A knifing won't help trade, will it? So get sensible. Pay me to leave and I'll go."

The one with the knife stood behind Ivy, holding her around the waist. He had the weapon at her throat. Evelyn's heart was going like the clappers. Her hands shook so much she could barely hold onto the dog. Her worst nightmare had just been made real.

"He'll use that knife, lady. You'd better hurry up."

"There is no money!" Evelyn screamed. "Come away from Ivy. Put down the vase. Leave the estate, and I promise we won't say anything."

The lad with the knife brandished it in front of Ivy's face. She screamed, Evelyn too.

"I'm not scared. I will cut her. You too. Serves you both right."

Evelyn didn't doubt him for a moment. The lad was hell bent on trouble.

Suddenly a deep male voice boomed out from the doorway. "Do as Lady Evelyn tells you, lad. Put the vase on the floor and be very careful. One chip, and I'll have your bollocks."

Evelyn spun round and saw a stranger. Whoever he was, he'd arrived just in the nick of time. The two lads took one look and visibly shrank, terrified. The man confronting them was about her own age — tall, still handsome despite his bulk, with flecks of grey in his dark hair and a scar high on his right cheek.

The scruffy lad stared at the man for a second or two, and then, much to Evelyn's surprise, he gently put the vase on the floor and backed away. He and his friend walked warily towards the door.

"Collect your friends from the fairground and leave quietly. Return, and you'll suffer the consequences. Get my drift, lad?"

A vigorous nod. "Sorry. Meant no harm."

"Before you leave, apologise to the ladies." The man smiled at the two frightened women. "Go on, or I'll take that knife and do you some damage myself!"

Seconds later, after a profuse apology, they were gone. Close to tears, Evelyn heaved a huge sigh of relief. "Oh, thank you! I dread to think what would have happened if you hadn't arrived."

"The door was wide open," he said. "I was on my way to the hall for a look around and saw what was happening. They won't trouble you again."

"I must call the police," Evelyn said. "Perhaps we should have tried to keep them here, then they could have been arrested."

The man shook his head. "They'll be gone by now. They've had a fright. Lads like them don't expect folk to fight back. They won't dare return."

He was probably right. They were gone now anyway, that was relief enough. She held out her hand. "I'm Evelyn Brindle."

He winked, took the proffered hand and kissed it. "I'm Jack. Jack Flanagan. You look as if you could do with a stiff drink."

"There's some brandy in our part of the house. Come through. You too, Ivy."

"I'm not alone," Jack said. "I came with some friends. You girls have your brandy, and take it easy. My friends and I'll have a wander round, and make sure all is well."

"I'd like to reward you in some way," Evelyn said. "You've saved our lives — not to mention the Moorcroft."

"It's an early one too." Carefully, he picked it up from the floor and handed it to her. "But I will claim my reward. Have dinner with me tonight. Suppose I pick you up at eight, alright? I know a nice little restaurant in town."

Though ordinarily Evelyn would never dream of going anywhere with a man she didn't know, this one had just saved the day. She smiled back. "Yes, I'd love that."

Chapter 14

Matt showed the photo of the anklet to Kate. "It's just a cheap piece of tat," she said. "I've seen stuff just like it on the market stalls in town."

"Why would something like this come with a job of work?"

She shrugged. "No idea."

"We need to find out. It might be important. We'll search the girl's bedroom this morning, and see what turns up."

Lily had finished interviewing the residents of Westgate, and was now at her desk looking at the CCTV footage she'd gathered. It wasn't much, but the most important came from a house across the road from the murder scene. Lily had been watching it on her computer and had frozen the film at a particular point.

"Sir!" she called out. "You should see this."

It showed Mary Salter leaving the house.

"We know she was there, she admitted as much," Matt said. "Does the camera show anything of Francine? She says she walked in on them arguing, and walked straight out again."

"Yes," Lily said. "She was telling the truth on that score. The camera picked her up about five minutes before this. She was in there a few seconds, tops. But the interesting bit about the Salter visit is just there." Lily pointed to the screen. Just visible behind the net curtain in the sitting room was the shadowy figure of a man. He appeared to be watching Mary leave.

"Ronald Potter?" Matt asked. "If that is him, then it's proof that neither Mary nor Francine is our killer. Good work, Lily. Ask the technicians if they can clean that piece of film up a bit. A good look at the man's face would be brilliant."

It still didn't help the case though. They might rule out Francine and Mary Salter, but they had no one else. Nor did they have a motive, apart from keeping the bodies from being found.

The case needed cranking up a bit.

He turned to Kate. "Did you find anything interesting on the previous tenants?"

"Most of them were local, and they all check out."

"There is still a question mark over those girls who were sharing. I rang Mary Salter, and she is still sketchy about the details. I'm going into the office later to follow up. Potter must have kept records."

"Pin Salter down. We need to know if they or any of the others had people staying with them during the time they were there. The same man has owned that house for the last twenty years, and he's never lived in it. It's always been let. There has to be something. We just haven't found it yet. Lily, you can come to the Fletcher house with me."

They were walking towards Matt's car when his mobile rang. It was his sister, Sarah.

"There was a nasty incident at the house this morning. Two ruffians with a knife threatened Mum and Ivy. They wanted money and said they'd tear the main hall apart if they didn't get it."

Matt stood stock still. He took a deep breath. This was just what his mother had been afraid of. "How are they?" His heart thumped loudly in his chest as he waited for her to reply.

"They're both fine, although Ivy has had to go home for a lie-down. But Mum has surprised me. I expected the usual — you know, the moans and recriminations — but she's quite chipper. Some man chanced by and scared the lads off. Mum reckons he saved their lives. A bit melodramatic, but you know what she's like. She's having dinner with him tonight."

"Didn't anyone think to ring the police?" Matt was astonished that no one had taken any action.

"No. Mum was happy to go with what Jack told her."

"Jack who? What's his full name? It all sounds a bit odd to me. Most folk would have been on the phone to the police at once."

"Mum won't hear a word against him. Apparently he's charming, and very good looking. I think Mum is a bit smitten. You'll see for yourself later when he picks her up. His name is Jack Flanagan. He's some sort of businessman."

Matt handed Lily the car keys. "Give me a minute, can you? I want a quick word with Kate before I go anywhere."

He hurried back into the building and went straight to the incident room. "You told me yesterday that your brother had had a tip-off that there'd be trouble at our event."

Kate nodded. "That's what Zane said."

"Who did it come from?"

"I've no idea. Like I said, he's young, and I'm afraid he has a liking for outlaws." She gave a caustic laugh. "I guess he finds them exciting. I hope he grows out of it."

"Ask him, will you? My mother was threatened this morning. Not just that, the man who came to her rescue was a stranger who appeared just in the nick of time. Much too convenient if you ask me."

"I will, sir. I'll speak to him later."

* * *

Christine Fletcher took the two detectives to her daughter's room. "I haven't touched anything, but it's in a bit of a mess. She has to share the room with our Kian, and I'm afraid his stuff is all over the place."

She left, pulling the door to behind her.

"What are we looking for, sir?" Lily asked.

"Anything that tells us what Karen was planning. She wanted a job. She might have gone for an interview."

"Her phone is on the table next to the bed. Odd she didn't take it with her." Lily bagged it. "She also has a laptop, sir." Lily pressed the 'on' button. "There's a load of stuff on here. Emails, Facebook messages, it needs looking at properly."

"We'll take it with us."

Matt found a business card lying on the dressing table. It was printed in shiny black and the logo was a cartoon image of a girl serving drinks on a tray. He read it out. "The Red Stiletto Club."

Lily snorted. "That dive? It's down a back street in the fag-end of Huddersfield — a casino and pole dancing club with a dubious reputation."

"So, what's their card doing in a sixteen-year-old's bedroom?"

Lily looked up at him from the laptop. "You don't think that's where she was thinking of working?"

Matt shrugged. "Well, she's underage for a start."

"That club was raided twelve months ago, and half the girls rounded up were underage. The club was fined and warned, but what's the betting they've carried on regardless? Karen's browsing history will tell us when we examine it. If she was planning to work in that club, there'll be emails. She'll have looked at the website."

"We'll go down there and take a look." Matt put the card in an evidence bag. "I can't see anything else. You?"

Lily was rooting around in the bedside cabinet drawers. She took out a large envelope addressed to Karen and handed it to Matt. "Sir, there's money in this."

The notes were fifties, all new and still in their plastic bags, fresh from the bank. A quick check showed that the serial numbers were consecutive. "There's about two grand here," he told Lily. "Where does a girl like Karen Fletcher get this much money from?"

Lily shrugged. "Tips?"

"Not this little lot. We'll ask her mother."

Christine Fletcher was waiting for them downstairs. She put a finger to her lips. The infant was sleeping in his pram.

"Are you any closer to finding her?"

Matt smiled. "A little, but we need longer to check a few details. The minute we know anything for sure, I'll tell you. We found a large amount of cash in Karen's drawer. Do you have any idea where she got it?"

Christine Fletcher looked surprised. "Kaz was always broke. She never had a bean. I provide most of what's needed for Kian." She nodded at the package. "That came in the post. I put it in the drawer for when Kaz returned."

"We'll keep it as evidence for the time being. We do need to know where it came from."

Christine Fletcher nodded reluctantly. "We could do with a windfall right now. The kid needs stuff."

"If Karen came by it honestly, she'll get it back," Matt said.

"I had Pamela Ansel from the hostel on the phone earlier, asking if she'd turned up. She's getting worried. Kaz hasn't been near the hostel, hasn't even texted her. Her and Pamela used to chat a lot."

Matt looked at Lily. "We'll check everything and I'll let you know what we find." They took the money, phone and laptop, and left the house quietly. The infant was still sleeping.

"We should speak to Pamela Ansel," Matt said when they were outside. "She reckons she hasn't seen Karen, but we shouldn't take that as gospel. We need a statement. We also need to check with the local banks, and find out which one issued those notes, and to whom. Pull Karen's phone records too. We need to know who she spoke to."

"I'll do that straight away," Lily said.

Matt heard his mobile beep. The message was from Graham Harwood at Pennine Forensics. He wanted to see him urgently.

"Okay, you go to the hostel in Huddersfield. Kate can visit the club. I've got to go and have a word with forensics."

* * *

The women's hostel was on the outskirts of Huddersfield. It was housed in an old Victorian semi that was long past its heyday. The place looked busy. A number of women were milling around at the front door.

One of them called out to Lily. "There's no room here, love! And there's a queue."

"It's okay," Lily said. "I'm just looking for Pamela Ansel."

The woman nodded to the door. "In there. Be warned — she's in a bad mood."

Lily went inside. The interior was depressing, with dark paintwork and small windows that let in little light.

"Can I help?" A woman was calling to her. "We don't allow people to just wander in off the streets."

"I'm not just wandering in. I'm looking for the manager."

"That's me. Pamela Ansel. What do you want?"

Lily introduced herself. "I'm trying to find Karen Fletcher."

"So is half the town. The silly girl has done one again. It's becoming a habit with her."

"Have you any idea where she might have gone?"

"Nope. The truth is, although she leant on this place at one time, I didn't really know Kaz that well. You should ask her mother, or that brother of hers."

"Did she have any friends here? Is there anyone you can think of that she might have gone to?"

The woman shook her head. "Sorry, we never got that close. I'm just a stopgap in their hard young lives. They don't confide in me."

Lily thought that was odd. Karen's mother had said the two of them spoke and texted a lot. Was Pamela Ansel hiding something? Lily needed to get straight onto Karen's mobile phone records.

"We think Karen was looking for work. Did she discuss that with you?"

"No. Why would she? I just want them back home where they belong. Her mother was happy to take her back, so job done. Karen ceased to be my responsibility."

"I get the impression that Karen wasn't all that happy at home. Have you any idea why that was?"

Pamela Ansel snorted. "You've met her mother? Enough to drive anyone away, that one.

"Here's my card. If you see Karen or she gets in touch with you, let me know."

Chapter 15

It was mid-afternoon and the club was closed, so Kate went round the back. Steam was billowing out of an open door and she could hear a man swearing.

"Problem?" She stood in the entrance, her warrant card ready in her hand.

"Bloody oven's on the blink again. Don't know how they expect me to cook with equipment from the ark."

"Is the manager around?"

The man's eyes narrowed. He turned away from the oven and looked her up and down. "He's not taking on."

"I don't want a job, just a chat." Kate thrust the warrant card in his face. "Now is he here, or do I come back later when the place is open?"

She saw his eyes dart to the uniformed officer standing behind her. "Leave him out there. He'll get the place a bad name." The man shuffled off, returning within minutes.

"Mr Lomax will see you in there." He pointed the way.

Kate walked along a dark passageway to the main bar area of the club. The dim lighting hid the sorry state of the place, but not enough. A pungent smell of booze and old cigarette smoke hung in the air. Most of the tables and upholstered seating were stained with the marks of spilled drink. Kate shuddered. She couldn't imagine why anyone would come here. Then she recalled her younger years, and how most nights she'd gone out around the backstreet clubs of Manchester. They hadn't exactly sparkled in the cold light of day either. She smiled to herself, wondering what had possessed her.

Lomax was sitting at a table, poring over some paperwork. Despite the early hour, he had a whiskey beside him. He was young, not much older than her, smartly dressed and not bad looking.

"I'm the manager, Martin Lomax. Accountants! A plague on every one of them." He pushed the papers to one side and smiled at her. "What's this about?"

The name didn't ring any bells. She'd have to ask the DI when she returned to the station. "Have you seen this girl recently?" She showed him the photo of Karen Fletcher.

He shook his head. "No idea, love. These girls, they come and go. They ask for jobs, and some I take on, most I don't. None of them stay very long. To be honest, once they get in the gear, they all look the same to me."

"Take another look. This is important. She's missing."

"Doesn't surprise me. Half the girls who work here are running from something."

"Talking of the gear the girls wear, do you give them these?" She showed him the image of the anklet.

"Yes. They have a black heart with the image of a red shoe in the middle. It's the club logo." He smiled. "The more popular the girl is, the more charms she gets. Every now and again there's a vote. As for the rest, we issue a complete uniform to our dancers — black spandex, with red stilettoes. Like them all to look the same. Same dance costume, blonde wig if their hair is a different colour.

Hang on and Lisa'll be out soon, so you can see for yourself. She likes to get in plenty of practice."

"Martin!" A female voice called from the stage. "This place is getting worse. It's bloody well infested with rats. I've just seen another one in the dressing room! You need to get someone in."

Kate turned. The girl was young, with long blonde hair cascading down her back. She was skimpily dressed and had the longest legs Kate had ever seen.

"Lisa is currently our number one pole dancer," Lomax said. "The punters come in their droves to watch her. The kid has a great future — providing she stops irritating everybody."

Kate couldn't get her head around the notion of choosing pole dancing as a career. But she had to admit, the girl was good. Lisa had put on some music and was practising her routine on one of the poles on stage. The moves she made would have put a gymnast to shame.

"I've got a man coming in tomorrow," Lomax shouted to her. "He'll sort the problem. Meanwhile, just go easy. No leaving food or booze hanging about."

Kate moved closer to the girl. She was wearing an anklet exactly the same as the one that had been found, but the one she wore must have had half a dozen or more charms on it. "Can I have a word?" she asked. "Do you know this girl?" Kate passed her the picture of Karen.

"Yeah, that's Kaz," she said at once. "Silly cow wanted to work here. I told her she was better off out of it. She wasn't the type, plus she's underage."

"Have you seen her recently?"

"No. She came here a while back and asked Martin for a job. Said she'd heard we were taking on. Martin sent her packing. Poor girl was nothing special. Hard to take, but true."

"How did she know there were jobs here?"

"No idea, love, didn't ask. The best bet around here is to mind your own business. Learnt that one a long time ago."

Kate walked back to Lomax. "Karen Fletcher thought you were taking on. Who would know that?"

He shrugged. "Anybody. One of the punters perhaps, or the girls. Truth is, we're always taking on. Our turnover is pretty brisk." He grimaced. "We're not the top club around. The girls get a bit of experience and then move on."

"Apart from the girls, who else might have one of these?" She showed him the photo of the anklet again.

"She might have found it. Got given it by one of our ex-dancers. So, anyone, is your answer."

Martin Lomax was pleasant enough, but Kate suspected he was hiding something. The man was well used to underhand practices. He ran this place for a start. Kate wasn't daft. In a side room, hidden by a curtain, she could see gaming machines and a table with a roulette wheel. People gambled here.

Lomax must have seen her glance. "We have a valid licence, you know. Everything is in order. We wouldn't be that stupid."

"We'll have to interview your other employees, Mr Lomax. We'll be in contact."

* * *

"Bit close for comfort that, Lisa. After what happened, the last thing we need is the coppers asking questions." Martin Lomax poured himself more whiskey and reached for his mobile. "Have a word with the other girls. And you don't say a word to anyone apart from them, got it? No mention of what happened, and no mention of Pam."

Lisa nodded.

Lomax put the phone to his ear. "A woman copper has just paid us a visit. She asked about the girl you sent, that Kaz. We have to get this right. She never came here. You never sent her. Got it? Keep it simple, and it'll save us a lot of aggro further down the line."

"They've been to the hostel too," Pamela Ansel said. "Sent by that whining mother of hers. I told them I hadn't seen the girl in a while."

"The police will get fed up soon and stop looking. As far as we're concerned, she's just another runaway."

Martin Lomax ended the call and looked around the room. If the police came back when they were open, the punters wouldn't be happy. He doubted they'd say anything, but several regulars had been in that night and had witnessed what had happened.

"We stick to the story. Have you got that, Lisa?"

She nodded. "I'll speak to the other girls, but a couple have left since that night."

"Do we have addresses?"

"Don't be soft, Martin. We don't even have proper names."

* * *

Doctor Graham Harwood was looking pleased with himself. "We've gone over that cellar inch by inch," he assured Matt. "There was so much dust and burnt material that I didn't expect to find much, but we struck lucky." He pointed to a dish containing what looked like melted plastic and paper. "It's what's left of a pack of sandwiches, cheese to be precise. See the paper?" Graham handed him a magnifying glass and turned the desk lamp onto it. "That's what's left of the label. We've cleaned it up, and you can just make out the sell-by date."

"Only ten days ago," Matt said. "The state of those bones, I imagined the poor girl had been dead a lot longer."

"Burning made it difficult to judge," Graham Harwood said. "But with this and the scrap of newspaper we found, we can be pretty sure that she died between ten days and two weeks ago."

"Surely the burning didn't take place in that cellar?" Matt said. "There'd be smoke and a smell. People would notice."

"I would say she was burnt somewhere nearby. Possibly in one of those garden rubbish incinerators, although we haven't found one. Whoever did this dismembered her body and burned the parts separately, some parts more than once. The bone, ash and everything else was then dumped on the cellar floor."

"He wanted to ensure she wasn't identified?"

"Possibly, but he wasn't consistent," Graham said.

"The carton, where did you find it?" Matt asked.

"In one corner, near the metal cover. Luckily for us it got covered in soot and dust, so the killer must have missed it."

"Any chance of fingerprints?" Matt said.

"Unlikely, but we'll certainly try."

"What about the head?"

"She was struck several times with something heavy. There are numerous cracks and holes in the skull. No chance of an ID from the head, I'm afraid."

"Thanks, Graham. No ID, but your hard work has given us a time frame. I'll go and update the team."

Chapter 16

Matt would hold a case meeting in the morning. Now, he needed to get off. Tonight, his mother was going out with a man she'd met only hours before, and he wanted to get a look at this hero who'd saved the day.

"She's in her room, preening." Sarah said when he got home. "My advice is, don't even try to put her off. She won't hear a word against him. And to be fair, if he hadn't turned up, the outcome could have been very different."

Matt shook his head. "I think you've all been taken in. I smell a set-up. My new DS's kid brother got a tip-off that there would be trouble at the fair. Hence my concern."

"Probably just a coincidence," Sarah said. "Besides, a night out can't do any harm, can it? She's not a child. We can't confine Mum to her room."

The thought of this made Matt laugh.

"You're not jealous, are you?" Sarah said, surprising him.

"Course not. I'm worried, sis. We don't know this man. For all we know, he could be behind what happened."

Sarah looked doubtful. "Why would he do that?"

"I've no idea. But I intend to find out."

Just then, Evelyn entered the room. Their mother looked lovely. She wore a cocktail dress of midnight blue silk that showed off her shapely figure.

"Looking good, Mum," Sarah said.

Evelyn looked at Matt, her expression grim. "Your sister told you the sorry tale?"

"Yes, and all about our hero."

"I know that look, son. Jack and I are going out for dinner. He invited me and after what he did, how could I refuse?" She smiled. "Don't read too much into it. He saved our lives. Me and Ivy were scared witless. Jack turned up and dealt with the two reprobates. He seems like a good man."

"They were trying to steal one of the vases?"

"Well they didn't succeed, thanks to Jack."

"Which one?" Matt asked.

"The tall green one in the side cabinet."

"Did he touch it? Jack, I mean."

"Yes, I think he did. Why all the questions, son? He is a thoroughly pleasant man. It's dinner, that's all. Just a meal."

Sarah had been peering through the window. "There's a large black limo coming up the drive. It appears he's got a chauffeur. He must be rich." She looked at Evelyn. "You've fallen on your feet here, Mum."

Evelyn looked pleased. "Don't be ridiculous."

Matt went to the front door to get a look at Jack Flanagan, but he was disappointed. Jack hadn't come himself, he'd sent his driver to pick up his mother.

"Mr Flanagan sends his apologies. A last minute business meeting he couldn't get out of. He is waiting for the good lady at the restaurant."

"My mother is through here."

The driver followed Matt into the main hall.

"Flanagan will meet you there, Ma," Matt told her. "Some hitch or other, so he couldn't come in person."

This didn't appear to bother Evelyn. She grabbed her coat and bag and set off after the driver. "Don't wait up! I'm a big girl now."

Matt followed them out into the hall. "What is Mr Flanagan's line of business?"

"He has interests in a number of companies," the driver said.

"Anything local?"

"I am employed to drive Mr Flanagan. I'm afraid I am not privy to other areas of his life."

Matt ran his hand through his short hair. He wasn't going to get anywhere, it was clear. His mother was glowering at him.

"Enjoy yourself, Ma." Matt nodded at the driver.

"You couldn't have sounded more suspicious if you'd tried," his sister hissed at him. "Let her be. Best fun she's had in ages."

Matt didn't agree. There was something going on, but he couldn't put his finger on it. Something about this man Flanagan wasn't right. Why hadn't he come to pick her up in person? What was he trying to hide? Matt was torn, and didn't know what to think. Like his mother had said, it was only dinner. For the sake of family peace, he would have to let it go.

"I'm going home," Sarah decided. "And despite what you think, I bet she sees him again."

"Hope not," Matt said. "The man's shifty."

"You've never even met him!"

But Matt knew he wasn't wrong. He couldn't get rid of the feeling that the entire incident had been engineered. The lads, then Flanagan stepping in and saving the day. One thing was for sure, he intended to find out a lot more about this man. He'd take the Moorcroft and get it checked for fingerprints. That way he'd know who the two ruffians were, and it might throw up something about the enigmatic Mr Flanagan.

He was about to take a walk around the fair, to carry out his nightly check, when his mobile rang. It was Kate Baxter.

"I went to the Red Stiletto Club earlier. I interviewed the manager and spoke to one of the girls. The manager is a man called Martin Lomax. I wondered if the name rang any bells. I got the distinct feeling he was hiding something. In fact, the whole place looked dodgy to me."

"Off the top of my head, no, I don't know the name. Check him out tomorrow when you're in the office. Get a profile of him up on the board."

"The dancers all wear the same anklet as the one that was found on the body. He couldn't say who the girl might be. As far as he is concerned, they come and they go. My instinct told me there was a lot more he could have said, but he chose not to."

"If he has a past, then we'll lean on him. Did the girls have anything to add?"

"I spoke to one of them, and she followed the party line."

"Did she know Karen?"

"Said she'd asked for a job at the club."

"Was she being truthful?"

"She might know more, but with her boss within earshot it was difficult for her to talk."

"We'll speak to Lomax again once we have his history."

As soon as Kate rang off, Talbot called.

"Is your mother there?" What to tell him? "It's about the play that's on in town. Wondered what night to get tickets for."

Talbot had a thing for his mother, Matt knew. He wasn't going to like the idea of her seeing another man.

"Er, she's gone out to dinner," he said.

"Who with? Your Sarah?"

"No. Someone she met recently."

"A man then." Down the line, Talbot sighed heavily. "Damn the woman. She knows how I feel. Hope he treats her right. Tell her I rang, will you? If she's interested, she can get in touch."

Talbot rang off, his voice heavy with disappointment. It was time for Matt to take the dog for his nightly jaunt around the fair. By this time tomorrow, it would have packed up and left. From what he'd seen of the figures, they'd done well out of the deal. Trade was up all round. The only fly in the ointment was the trouble his mother had suffered. Matt was still convinced that it was a put-up job.

Everything at the fairground looked fine. It was still daylight, and the place was full of families. Matt saw a familiar face by one of the ice cream vans — Denny Clarke. Denny was an informant that DC Ian Beckwith often used. What, Matt wondered, was he doing here?

Matt strolled over to him. "A bit far out for you, Denny."

"Just seeing how the other half live. Like your place. Big, innit? Bet it takes some keeping up."

Matt laughed. "You're not wrong there. That's partly what this event is all about, raising money."

"Things okay, are they?" Denny was shuffling around, looking down at his feet, and avoiding eye contact. "After what happened, you know, the robbery?"

"There was no robbery, Denny. We were lucky. A passing visitor stepped in and did his hero bit."

"So I heard," Denny said. "But things aren't always as they seem, are they?"

"What do you mean? What do you know about it?"

Denny looked up at him. "It'll cost you. Bloke who lives in a house like that," he nodded at the Brindle mansion, "you might need money, but I bet you're still worth a bob or two."

"Is this police business?" Matt asked.

"Might be. Then again, it might be personal."

Matt was intrigued. "What do you mean?"

"Look, give me twenty and I'll tell you what I know."

Denny had obviously come here tonight expecting to cut a deal. Matt stuck his hand in his pocket and took out two tenners. "Come on then, what was the incident all about?"

"If you think it was a set-up, you're right. That bloke who sorted them villains paid them to do it. The plan was he'd turn up just at the right moment and sort 'em."

Matt had known it all along. "How did you get to hear about this?"

"I heard a whisper. I don't know any more." Denny began to sidle away.

"I think you do, Denny. I think you know who the man is, for a start. He calls himself Jack Flanagan, but that's not his real name, is it?"

Denny Clarke shook his head. "More than my life's worth. Tell you, and I'm a dead man."

So that was the reason he'd sent his driver to the house and hadn't come himself. The man must have been afraid that Matt would recognise him. "Do I know him?"

"He's not a man to get involved with. Warn your mother. Tell her to watch her step. That man is ruthless. A killer."

Matt looked away for a moment. A girl on one of the rides had screamed and the noise frightened the dog, making it pull on the lead. When he looked back, Denny Clarke had done one.

Chapter 17

Day 5

Matt was in the incident room early the next morning. He hadn't spoken to his mother about her date. When he'd left the house she was still asleep. He sat at one of the computers and did a database search for Jack Flanagan, not expecting to find anything.

And he was right, there was nothing. Matt was sure the man was dodgy, so he'd either been extremely careful all his life or there was something amiss. Matt wracked his brain. He had to find out who this man really was. When Lily arrived, so intent was he on ploughing through the database that he didn't notice her come in. Her voice in the background was just so much white noise. All he was aware of was the information on the screen, not that it was any help.

"A call, sir." Lily was holding the office phone out to him. "She says she wants to speak to DS Baxter, but she's not here yet."

"Can't you deal with it?"

"She won't speak to anyone but Kate, or the person in charge."

Reluctantly, Matt took the phone from her. The caller told him her name was Lisa and that she worked at the Red Stiletto.

"I have to speak to someone about the girls. It's very important, and it won't wait."

This was the girl Kate had told him about. "DS Baxter will come and see you later," Matt said.

"No! She mustn't come here. Lomax will guess that I've spoken to you. It'll have to be somewhere else. The café by Marsden railway station in half an hour." She rang off.

"I've been onto the banks, sir," Lily said. "They're checking the numbers and will get back to us."

Matt hardly heard. He jotted down the information from Lisa, carefully picked up the Moorcroft vase and left the incident room. Inside the main office, he collared one of the uniformed officers.

"I want this transported to forensics very carefully. It's covered in fingerprints, and I don't want them obliterated or smudged. I'll ring and tell them to expect you."

He'd wanted to take it himself, but he had to go and speak to Lisa. Apart from possibly knowing something about the girls, particularly Karen Fletcher, she might give them some information about Martin Lomax.

Matt was passing Talbot's open door on his way back to the incident room when the super called him in. Matt found him sitting behind his desk, tucking into a bacon barm.

"Bloody good fodder in that canteen of ours. You should get yourself one. Put a smile on that long face of yours."

"My mother is seeing a man called Jack Flanagan," Matt said flatly. "He's a villain, but I can't find any trace of him, so Flanagan can't be his real name."

Talbot's bun was halfway to his mouth. He put it down. "How does that happen? How did Evelyn manage to get herself involved with a villain?"

"Because he's clever. He's masquerading as a businessman. Yesterday he turned up just in time to save my mother and Ivy from two lads hell bent on mayhem. Now Ma thinks he's wonderful. She had dinner with him last night. God knows what he wants. But there will be something behind it, mark my words."

"Did you meet him?"

"No, he sent his driver to pick her up. Now I know why. He must have guessed I'd recognise him."

"What d'you want me to do? Talk to her?"

Matt shook his head. "I'm not sure she'd listen. I suspect he isn't going to go away. I want to know what he wants. I know you're fond of my mother, and you'd be concerned as well."

There was an awkward silence. "True, I am fond of her, lad," Talbot said, "but if she likes him, what can either of us do?"

"You can help me find out his true identity for a start. He touched one of the vases the lads were about to steal. I've sent it to forensics. His prints might be on record. If anyone asks, it's to do with our current case, okay?"

"Good call, lad. Tell them it's a rush job, stuff the cost."

"I'll get back to work then."

Talbot returned to his breakfast.

* * *

He went back to the incident room, where Lily told him that DS Baxter had just rung in sick.

"She was fine yesterday." Right now, Matt had very little sympathy.

"Reckons it was something she ate," Lily said. "Hopefully she'll be back tomorrow."

Matt looked at the note he'd left for her. No Kate, so he would have to go and meet with this Lisa by himself.

"This morning, I want you to find out all you can about the Red Stiletto Club and its manager, Martin Lomax." Lily's eyebrows rose. This obviously sparked her interest. "Then I want you to visit Mary Salter again, and ask her about the last tenants, the young women. We need those names, their forwarding addresses, and the names of any referees they may have given."

"Are you sure, sir? I don't want to step on DS Baxter's toes."

"Well, she's not here, is she?"

Matt took his jacket from the back of his chair and left. He'd meet with Lisa first, and then he *had* to go home and speak to his mother. Perhaps this so-called Flanagan had said something to her that would prove useful.

* * *

Kate Baxter tugged at her brother's duvet. "Zane! Come on, it's time to wake up. I have a job to go to, but first we need to talk. You were out until all hours again last night. You're supposed to be grounded — remember?"

The lad didn't stir. He'd staggered in during the early hours, off his head on something. He had a nasty gash on his temple and was bleeding from a wound on his leg. Kate had wanted to clean him up then, but he'd flopped onto his bed and passed out, so she'd left him to it. This wasn't the first time, and it wouldn't be the last.

But in the cold light of day, it was obvious that something was seriously wrong. He was unconscious, very pale, and she was worried. "Zane? Are you okay? Are you with it, bro?"

There was no response. Gently, Kate lifted the duvet and took a closer look at his leg. Blood had soaked the sheet and seeped through to the mattress. Her brother was more badly wounded than she'd thought last night. From the bruises on his face and that gash, he must have been attacked. The leg could be a stab wound.

Kate grabbed her phone and rang for an ambulance. While she waited, she went through his pockets, looking for any hint as to what he might have been up to the night before. There were several wraps of what she took to be weed, a bit of loose change and a business card. The Red Stiletto Club. Her heart sank. What had possessed him to go there?

Not only were they employing underage girls, but the door staff were obviously only too willing to beat up young lads. Martin Lomax would get another visit, and it wouldn't be pleasant.

She heard Zane's mobile trill, and she answered it. It was his friend, Caleb.

"How's he doing? He looked pretty bad last night."

"He's unconscious. He's been badly beaten. Why did you go to that club? And what the hell happened to him?"

"He asked the wrong person one question too many."

"What question? And what did you hope to gain by going there?"

"We were looking for my sister, Kaz. She worked there."

"Karen Fletcher is your *sister*?" Kate was surprised and also annoyed with herself that she hadn't cottoned on when she heard his name the first time.

"Yeah, and she's missing. Has been for days. You lot aren't doing anything, so we thought we'd have a go. That bastard Lomax is at the bottom of it. Our Kaz isn't the only girl from there to disappear either. There's another one, Caroline Perks. No one has seen her in weeks."

The name was new. She thought of the bones, the body parts. The Fletcher lad's information could be important.

"I'll get Zane sorted, and then we'll talk. You can tell me about Karen and Caroline. I take it you will make a statement?"

"Don't want my head kicking in," he said.

"But you do want us to find your sister. You can't have it both ways, Caleb. You help us, we'll help you."

* * *

"I wanted to speak to that woman detective."

"Too bad, you've got me." Matt showed Lisa his ID. "What do you have to say?"

She frowned and shook her head. "How do I know I can trust you?"

"You'll just have to take that chance. But be warned. This is a murder enquiry. We have missing girls, and we've found a body. If you know something, you need to talk to me."

Matt was aware of how brusque he was being, but he couldn't help it. The problem with his mother and this Flanagan bloke, and why wanted into their lives was consuming all his thoughts.

The young woman eyed him suspiciously. "This mustn't get back to Lomax. If it does, I'm dead."

Matt nodded. "Do you know where Karen Fletcher is?"

"No. But she did work at the club. He told DS Baxter that we didn't know Kaz, but that's not true. She worked with us for a while. Then she left suddenly."

"Do you know why?"

"No. One night she didn't turn up, and that was it."

"How long did she work there?"

"Six months, maybe a bit more."

Matt was astonished. "But she's only sixteen now!"

"The younger they are the better, as far as Lomax is concerned. Brings in the punters. But what bothers me is that Kaz left after a blazing row with Lomax. I don't know what started it, but I think he paid her off. Now he denies ever knowing her. Then another girl, Amy, disappeared too, but unlike Kaz, she had no home to run to. Lomax said he'd take care of her, and we haven't seen her from that day to this."

"What do you think happened to her?"

"I have this horrible feeling that they were got rid of somehow. I think he threatened Kaz. I know she was scared stiff. The night of the argument she created quite a scene. Screamed her head off and accused Lomax of all sorts. I don't know what it was about, but another of the girls said it was to do with a girl called Caroline and her boyfriend. Why that should bother Kaz or Lomax I've no idea. This body you've found — a young woman, is it?"

Matt shook his head. "A dead estate agent," he said. He didn't want the find in the cellar getting out just yet. "When exactly did you last see Amy and Caroline?"

"Amy, about two weeks ago. She did her usual shift, left for the night and we haven't seen her since. She asked Caroline if there was a bed at hers, but Caroline wasn't keen. I have no idea if she helped Amy out or not. I haven't seen her for a week or so either."

"Where does this Caroline live?" Matt asked.

"Somewhere local I suppose. She was renting a house. Girls from the club would stay there from time to time."

"Who was the landlord?"

"I've no idea. It was probably dodgy anyway. I asked Lomax about Amy but he said she'd done one. I don't believe that. She had nowhere to go. Amy wouldn't survive on the streets, she's not tough enough."

"Could she have gone to the women's refuge, the one run by Pamela Ansel? Kaz was there for a while."

"Ansel is up to her eyes in it too. Don't trust a word she says."

Matt made a mental note to interview the woman as soon as possible.

Chapter 18

The work was piling up. Matt should go and speak to Pamela Ansel, perhaps even bring her in. But first he needed to go home and speak to his mother. She had to be warned, made to see reason. His head was too full of Flanagan to do much else, and he couldn't concentrate on the intricacies of the case.

It was a sunny day, the middle of the school holidays, and the Brindle estate was full of life. Matt's plans were bearing fruit. If it weren't for the worry of his mother, he'd be thrilled. But as it was, he had to sort the problem before it festered and grew into something much worse.

Ivy met him at the door. "If you're looking for Lady Evelyn, she isn't here. Jack rang earlier, then came and picked her up. They've gone to York races for the day."

Was there no end to this? "Did he come here — Flanagan?"

"Yes," Ivy said. "He met your sister. Turned on the charm. She liked him."

Matt shook his head. "None of you know him." He left the house and made for a café just beyond the formal gardens. The place was packed, and he had to pick his way carefully to the counter. Sarah was busy taking orders.

"What's Ma doing taking off with Flanagan again?" he barked at her.

"Tone it down," she said. "You're the last one who should be frightening the customers, after the struggle we've had to get them." She had a point. "She likes him, Matt, simple as that. She's like a teenager. I haven't seen her so happy in months. Jack Flanagan is a tonic. Done her the world of good."

"He's a villain."

He saw her look. Sarah didn't believe a word.

"Do you have proof of that?" she asked.

Reluctantly, Matt shook his head.

"He's just a businessman, he's doing no harm. And not in here, Matt, you're doing the atmosphere no good at all."

"I need a word," he hissed. "There's a lot you don't know."

"And I don't want to know. I don't understand what's got into you. The man is perfectly sound."

He was wasting his time. Flanagan had charmed the three of them, his mother, Sarah — even Ivy, the housekeeper. He'd need something more tangible before they'd take him seriously.

* * *

When Matt got back to the station, Kate was sitting at her desk.

"I thought you were ill," he said.

"I had a domestic problem. I didn't want to use that as an excuse, so I lied. Sorry."

Matt didn't like the sound of that. The workload was spread thin enough as it was. "Do you want to talk about it?"

"I'm going to have to. It affects the case we're working on."

Lily looked up from her computer screen.

"You'd better explain," Matt said.

"My brother Zane is pally with Caleb Fletcher, Karen's brother. I didn't realise that until very recently. Last night the two of them went to the Red Stiletto. I don't know the details of what happened, but Zane was attacked. He's in hospital with concussion and a stab wound to his left thigh. It was a vicious assault. He's had to have scans and a blood transfusion." She paused. "I had no idea they were going. Zane tells me bugger all about what he's up to. The two of them know nothing about our investigations. They went to the club because Caleb Fletcher knows that Karen worked there. He needs to be interviewed quickly, I think he can help. I only discovered all this earlier today, but I couldn't come in to work and tell you. When I saw the amount of blood Zane had lost overnight, it shocked me. I had to get him some help, find out how bad he was. I've been at the hospital since eight."

Matt had no answer to this. How could he criticise Kate when he'd just been home himself? He turned to Lily. "Did you discover anything about the club, or Lomax?"

"Not much. He's the manager, as we knew. The club is owned by one Paul Ainley."

The dead villain in the car. This was just too much of a coincidence. He'd no way of knowing how involved Ainley had been with the running of the club, but it was extremely suspicious. Ainley's death might even have been the result of a row between him and Lomax. Added to what had happened to Zane Baxter and what Lisa had told him, they had reason to bring Lomax in and search the place. "Give me a minute," he told the two women.

Matt went to Talbot's office and banged on his door. Talbot Dyson was seated behind his desk, sifting through a pile of paperwork.

"Paul Ainley, our dead villain, owned a club in town called the 'Red Stiletto' ".

"We know. It's a backstreet hole near the canal," Talbot said. "What of it?"

"We now have a connection between the missing girls, Karen Fletcher in particular, and the Red Stiletto. It's managed by one Martin Lomax. Do you know him?"

"He's been had up for a couple of offences in the past. But Ainley, he was good at covering his tracks. He had an interest in numerous businesses," Talbot said. "Most of them are legit."

"I doubt the Red Stiletto is. Given what we've got, I want to bring Lomax in and search the place. At the very least, he should be questioned about Ainley's death."

Talbot's face fell. "That is Carlisle's case. Exactly what have you got? I hope it's good, because Lomax has made complaints against the police in the past. Last time he accused us of being heavy handed when he was had up for employing underage girls in that dive of his."

"Leaving the Ainley factor to one side for the moment, one of the girls spoke to me earlier. She told me that a couple of the dancers have gone missing, Karen Fletcher for one. We've got a dead club owner, a dead estate agent, a pile of bones, female I might remind you, coupled with girls missing from that club. If bringing in Lomax upsets the powers that be or Carlisle, then so be it."

"I'm sure Lomax's solicitor will argue that he had nothing to do with any of that. He employs the girls, he isn't responsible for all their actions or who they get involved with. And as for Ainley, half the Huddersfield underground had a beef with him."

"You're saying we don't have enough?"

"I think you should err on the side of caution," Talbot said.

"At the very least, Lomax might throw some light on who Ainley had upset recently."

Talbot pursed his lips. Finally, he said, "I'm just trying to work out what it all means, if anything."

"Ainley and Lomax. A dodgy club. Girls work there and disappear, beatings at the door, and underage dancers. That enough for you?"

"Even so, a good solicitor will shoot you down in flames. And Carlisle will want in," Talbot said.

"But not yet. The girls are part of my enquiry, and it's Lomax I'm interested in, not Ainley. As for the solicitor, I'll take my chances."

"Okay," Talbot said, "I'll hold off giving Carlisle this new information. And understand that you bring Lomax in against my better judgement."

"Flanagan is still seeing my mother by the way. What do you reckon that's all about?"

"Respectability, lad. If, like you reckon, Flanagan is a villain, he could be thinking of giving up, going straight. He's looking for a country pile and a lady to go with it. It will give him a certain kudos that he doesn't currently have. Make people see the gent and not the dodgy businessman. I'm afraid Evelyn is a pawn in a long game. Of course, I could be wrong. It may be something to do with the family."

There was something in Talbot's tone that made Matt suspicious. "Do you know who he is?" he asked.

"No. Just thinking out loud." Talbot reached into his desk drawer for a file. "Keep me posted with regard to Lomax." Matt was dismissed.

But he wasn't convinced. Talbot was keeping something from him. "I'm bringing Lomax in this morning. I want to find out who killed Potter and what happened to those missing girls. Then I can concentrate on saving my mother from a load of grief." He stalked back to the incident room.

* * *

"We're going after Lomax," Matt told Kate and Lily. "Lily, round up half a dozen uniforms for backup."

"Can I be in on the interview, sir?" Kate asked.

"No. Your brother was at the club, and he got beaten up. You'll have to keep out of it. Lily will join me. You check with the banks again, hurry them up, and go to IT forensics. See what they've got from Karen's laptop. Did you check that the gaming licence was in order?"

"Yes, it's fine," Kate said.

"The uniforms will meet us at the club," Lily said to Matt.

"Are you bringing Lomax in on the basis of what happened to my brother?" Kate asked.

"Not entirely. Paul Ainley, the dead man in the car, owned that club. We need to speak to Lomax about him too. But based on what one of the dancers told me this morning, we have a lot more to discuss. Also, Lomax is still hiring underage girls. We'll check his employment records. Any discrepancies at all, and we throw the book at him."

Matt and Lily left the station and made for the car park. Matt was frowning, not in the mood for talking.

"Is something wrong, sir?" Lily asked. "You don't look happy, and I get the feeling it's more than just the case."

Matt didn't want to go into details, but she had asked. Plus, no one else would listen. "It's my mother, and it's complicated. She is hurtling headlong towards trouble, but she won't listen."

"A man then."

Matt gave Lily a sidelong glance. For someone so young, she was pretty clued up. "A man who I'm convinced is dodgy, but my mother has dug her heels in."

"Has it got something to do with the case?"

"I don't think so. His name is Jack Flanagan, supposedly. It's not one that's come up."

* * *

The Red Stiletto was in darkness. Matt peered through the letterbox, and then banged on the door. The pavement outside was littered with cigarette ends and other rubbish. Someone had tipped a dustbin upside down and its contents were blowing down the street.

"This place — the entire area in fact — is the pits," Lily said. "Why folk risk life and limb coming to this part of town after dark is beyond me."

But Matt wasn't listening. Riled up about recent events, he was banging on the window with his fist.

Chapter 19

"I need help!" The girl screamed. "You can't do this!"

She felt her way carefully around the confined space, trying to find the door in the dark. Her belly ached and she felt sick. She'd had very little to eat for days, and what little water was left in the bottle tasted funny.

"What do you want?" a woman called back at her.

"I don't feel right. I'm starving and my hands are sore." She couldn't see the wounds to her fingers but they hurt like hell. She'd done the best she could to bandage them with a hankie, but she needed proper treatment.

She shouted out again. She was really afraid now. These people were capable of anything. Thankfully, after a few moments the key turned in the door lock, and the girl heaved a sigh of relief.

"Come with me," the woman ordered. "Walk in front where I can see you, and don't try anything."

The ache in the girl's leg hadn't eased any, and climbing the steep stone steps was agony. Even in the semi gloom of the staircase, the black bruise on her right calf was evident. The blow with the poker had been vicious.

"I need a doctor. My fingers are infected after you ripped the nails off." She was angry. How long was this going to continue?

"I'll check you over and then we'll see."

The girl was taken to a room on the ground floor, furnished with a metal bed and medical equipment. It looked like a clinic.

"Sit down. I'll check your blood pressure."

"I can't stay in that cellar. You have to let me go. You have to believe me. I have no idea where Caroline is, I really haven't. She disappeared. *He* might know, Martin from the club. They got on well."

The woman wrapped the cuff around the girl's upper arm. "Shut it while I do this."

The girl looked at her surroundings. The door was ajar, and on the other side of the hallway she could see an open window. It was one of those old-fashioned sash ones. If she could get to it, push it open a little more, she had a chance of getting away.

Her captor referred to a chart on the desk. "It's higher than I'd like." Her face wore a frown, and from her tone the girl knew she was worried. "Stick this under your tongue, I'll take your temperature."

The girl took the thermometer, sat still and closed her eyes.

Several minutes passed. "Well?" she asked.

"It's high." The woman removed the hanky, which was filthy. "You do have an infection. Your finger looks septic. I did warn you what would happen."

"Let me go. I won't say anything."

"You're free to go when you've told me where Caroline is hiding."

The girl shook her head. "I don't know. Do you think I'd stay in this dump a minute longer than I needed to if I did?"

The girl watched the woman's face. She was considering this.

"Stay there. Don't try anything, or you'll come off worse. I'm going to make a call."

The woman left the room. The girl waited a while, then stood up and crept to the door. Her intention was to attempt her escape through the window, but she could barely move. Her leg hurt and her head was spinning. There'd be no second chance, though. She had to go now.

* * *

"I can't give you long. I'm a busy man, Inspector." Martin Lomax sat back in his chair and crossed his legs. "I have a club to run."

Matt Brindle was in no mood to listen to the man's excuses. He wanted answers. He and Lily sat opposite Lomax and his solicitor in an interview room. They had brought him in against Talbot's advice. The super had quite rightly pointed out that they had no actual evidence that would hold up in court. The fight in which Zane Baxter got hurt had nothing to do with Lomax. According to them, that was down to the doormen. As for the underage girls, Matt was chancing his arm. But it was too late for second thoughts.

"Have you seen this girl?" Matt pushed the image of Karen Fletcher across the desk.

Lomax leaned forward and studied it for a few moments. "No. I told your sergeant as much when she asked me about her before."

"You're lying. We now know that she worked for you until very recently." Matt paused momentarily. He'd expected his words to have more effect, but Lomax seemed unconcerned. His expression didn't change. "Her name is Karen Fletcher. She is missing, and we have found a body." That didn't appear to shake him either.

"That is tragic," Lomax said. "But it has nothing to do with me or the club. What those girls get up to in their own time is their business." He looked at the photo again. "The problem is, it's so difficult to tell. When the girls are done up in the costumes, they all look the same. Your information could be right. She might have worked for us, but I couldn't say for sure."

"We're not mistaken. Karen Fletcher worked for you alright. We have been given reliable information. What happened, Mr Lomax? Why did she leave and where did she go?"

"I have no idea. I don't keep track of their movements. All I'm interested in is that they turn up for work."

"There was an incident. You and Karen argued. Surely you remember that. She made quite a scene, I was told. Upset the customers. I'm sure we'll be able to find someone who will testify."

Lomax leaned toward his solicitor and whispered something in his ear.

"Speak to the customers," he said. "If you find one who remembers, you then have the task of getting them to give a statement. Unlikely, given our clientele." He smiled. "I have things to do. I don't have to sit here and listen to this."

"A young man was badly beaten outside your club last night. What happened?"

"Again, I have no idea. People drink too much, they get fired up. One wrong word and the sparks fly. You can hardly blame me or the club for that."

"It was your doormen who caused the injuries," Matt said. "The young man was asking about Karen Fletcher. Odd, don't you think?"

"Wrong word, wrong ear. Like I said, people drink, things get heated."

"You don't own the Red Stiletto, you simply manage it. Are you aware that the owner, Paul Ainley, was recently found murdered?"

Lomax nodded. "Bad business. I heard something about that on the radio. The next day I got a phone call from Paul's sister. She told me what had happened."

"What's your take on that, Mr Lomax? How did Paul Ainley end up burnt to death?"

"I can't help you there either. I rarely saw him. As I'm sure you already know, Paul didn't always stay the right side of the law. He made enemies. I suggest you look among them."

Lomax was far too smooth. "Exactly who are these enemies you're talking about?" Matt asked.

"I've no idea. Surely that is more your territory than mine?"

Another clever answer, another smile. "Does anyone else own a share of that club?"

"No, just Paul."

"In that case, you could lose your job, depending on Ainley's will and who inherits."

"It's likely that his sister will get the lot. The business makes a good income. I'm sure she'll want it to continue."

"You are very sure of that, Mr Lomax."

"The arrangement has already been discussed."

Matt shook his head. "How involved was Ainley in the day to day running of the place?"

"Like I said, we saw very little of him. He left everything up to me, including hiring and firing and initiatives to increase trade."

He was lying. Matt saw the shifty look he gave his solicitor. The mention of Ainley was making Lomax nervous. "Does the casino take much money?" Matt asked.

"We do alright. But folk don't have a lot of money to spend at the tables. It's more about having a flutter at the weekend. Nothing heavy, Inspector. No one gets into debt and even if they did, we'd work something out."

The man had an answer for everything. Time to hit him with the age of his staff. "You employ girls under the age of eighteen. As you well know, that is against the law."

"Really, Inspector, is that all you've got? Okay, I hold my hands up to that one," he said. "One or two do slip through the net. But what can I do? They certainly look old enough. We ask for ID but they rarely have any, and what we do get shown is often forged. To be honest, a lot of them are in a bad place, they're runaways. They need a job, the company of the other girls."

Matt snorted. "Oh, so you're social workers, is that what you're saying?"

"I take on the girls that show talent. Not all of them get through. After that, it's up to them. The pay is generous and the tips are good. If a girl has had a hard time, she is soon able to get back on her feet."

The only thing they had on this man was contravention of the employment laws. They had no proof that Karen Fletcher had come to any harm while in the club's employ, or that Zane Baxter had been deliberately attacked. Matt wanted to search the premises, interrogate Lomax's phone records, but without more, they wouldn't get a warrant.

"You will be charged with employing underage girls. It's not the first time, so no doubt the penalty will be steep." Matt stood up. "You can go. But we'll speak again."

Frustrated, Matt said nothing on the way back to the incident room. He'd wanted answers, but Lomax was slippery. They had to get more information, solid proof, if he was to be brought in again. Matt hated to admit it, but Talbot was right. He'd had a go at Lomax because he was angry about Flanagan and his mother. What was he thinking? He'd let his emotions get in the way. A bad mistake.

Back in the incident room, he rang Graham Harwood. "The case is going nowhere unless we get something from you guys. I have a suspect, someone who probably employed the dead girl, but I have nothing to pressure him with."

"We are still searching the house on Westgate. One thing, though. That residue we sampled from the door of the kitchen unit, we found a couple of hairs — blonde but fake, from a wig."

That checked out with what Kate had been told. All the girls at that club wore blonde wigs as part of their costumes. "Anything else?"

"We're still digging in the garden and lifting the stone flags in the cellar. If we find anything, I'll let you know."

Matt looked around. "Where is DS Baxter?"

"She has gone to IT forensics, sir," said a uniformed PC. "They rang about half an hour ago."

That was something at least.

Chapter 20

Karen Fletcher kicked at the front door. She had lost her key. She was cold, her teeth chattered, and her skinny arms were wrapped tight around her body for warmth. Her eyes had dark circles beneath them. She looked as if she hadn't slept in days.

Finally her mother appeared at the door. "At last!" Kaz said. "Where the hell have you been? I've been standing here for ages."

"Kaz! You're back!" Christine Fletcher exclaimed. "I've been so worried. I was thinking all sorts. I even thought you might be dead."

Brushing aside her mother's open arms, Karen hurried inside. "I will be if you don't help me." She limped into the kitchen and flicked the switch on the kettle. "Anything to eat? I'm starving. The last food I had was ages ago."

"What were you thinking, taking off like that?" her mother said. "I've had the police here, looking for you."

"Keep them out of my hair. I mean it, Mum." Her eyes were steely. "I can't talk to them."

"I have to tell them you've turned up, Kaz."

"No! Not yet. I'll stay here, under the radar. Folk ask, you tell them I'm still missing." The last thing Karen wanted was her mother shooting her mouth off. "No one must know. Do you understand?" Her face was set hard. She meant it.

Christine Fletcher shook her head. "You haven't asked about Kian."

Karen heaved a weary sigh. "Go on then, tell me."

"He cries all the time. He's more than I can handle. I'm too old to be looking after an infant. You might be in hiding, our Kaz, but now you're here you can do your share. He's your son, not mine, and I'm exhausted."

Karen wasn't listening. She'd buttered several slices of bread and spread them thickly with jam. "I'm having this, a bath then getting some sleep. You can manage till I wake up?" She eyed her mother suspiciously. "What did you tell the police? You didn't tell them about me working at the club, did you?"

"I told them I didn't know. But they found one of those anklet things and showed me a photo. I was worried sick. I said you'd had one too."

"Stupid cow! You'll get me done. If Lomax finds out you dobbed him in, I'm toast."

"I had the police and that social worker on my back. I had no idea where you were, and they've found a body. What was I supposed to do?" She paused. "I can't pretend you're still missing for long. You should speak to the police yourself."

"No! I daren't. Do you know what they do to folk who grass?"

Her mother sighed resignedly. "What have you got mixed up in, our Kaz?"

"Better you don't know."

"Where have you been these last few days anyway?"

"Hiding at a mate's house. I got into a bit of bother with some hard types." She shook her head. "I had no choice but to stay out of sight. It's over now."

"What *hard types*? Have you been messing with drugs again?"

"No, nowt like that. I overheard something at that club. There was a row. The bloke that runs it found out and wanted me gone. So I did one before stuff got heavy."

"What did you hear?"

"Safer for you if I say nowt."

"I told you not to go there. You're not old enough for a start."

"I have to work. We need the money. Babies don't come cheap. The club was the only place that'd employ me. But that's finished now. I won't be going back."

"The police searched your room. They found some money in an envelope. A lot of money, Kaz."

Karen spun round. "That money is mine. For me and Kian once things get sorted."

"They took it. I didn't know it was there. You should have trusted me, I would have hidden it. Where did it come from?"

"Never mind that! What do I do now it's gone? It was my one chance for a fresh start. You can't do anything right. Oh, I'm going to bed."

* * *

Talbot summoned Matt to his office. "It's as I feared. On advice from his solicitor, Martin Lomax is threatening to make a complaint! I told you we weren't ready. You should have left the man alone. We'll get what we need to prosecute in the end, but we still have a way to go."

"Meanwhile the man has carte blanche, does he? Runs that club exactly as he wants and we don't bat an eyelid? He is employing underage girls!" Matt slammed his fist down on Talbot's desk. "We know that at least one of them is missing, possibly more, and we haven't a clue. All we know is that Karen Fletcher got into bother at that club. I met with one of the girls. She confirms there was a row, but she's terrified of saying more. If any of those body parts turns out to belong to Karen Fletcher, what then?"

Talbot shook his head. He hadn't seen Matt Brindle so wound up since the murder of Paula Wright. "You need to cool down, Matt. This thing with your mother has gone to your head. You're not seeing straight."

"I want that place searched. I want Lomax's background investigated. He's involved in this up to his armpits, I know it. You swear by your own instinct, Talbot — don't you trust mine?"

"Without evidence, no, lad, it's not enough. We daren't risk it. Now get off home and calm down. This case has got to you. You need a night off."

"It has nothing to do with the case, Talbot. The way I am, how I feel is down to that man Flanagan. If I catch him at home, fawning over my mother, I'm likely to lose it."

"Nonetheless, you're not staying here. I want you gone. Get off to the pub if you must — but do one."

* * *

Slamming the door behind him, Matt strode out of Talbot's office. Back in the incident room, Lily was getting ready to go home.

"Fancy a drink? You look as if you could do with one."

"I'm no company," he told her. "Ring that boyfriend of yours. He's a much better choice. You don't want me stringing along in the mood I'm in."

"Greg is working late. So, mood or not, you're my only option, I'm afraid. Unless I want to sit at the bar like Billy No-mates."

Matt would have preferred to be left alone to stew in his black mood, despite knowing from experience that it wasn't good for him. He'd suffered from enough of them after the accident. "Okay, but just the one. I don't want to roll home legless."

"Might do you good. Not easy, is it, all this getting nowhere."

She was right. Matt managed to crack a smile. Lily was a good sort. They had spoken a little about her background, and Matt knew that things had been difficult for her. She hadn't always gotten along with her parents. Her father had left her and her mother, and her mother hadn't coped well. She drank a lot so Lily said. She'd been lucky, though. Her grandparents had watched her back.

They set off for the pub. On the way, she asked, "Do you reckon one of those bodies is Karen Fletcher?"

"Difficult to say. Could be. She ran away, and that can be dangerous. If you don't have anyone to run to, things get tricky. We all know what it's like out there. A young girl, if she's living rough, she'll be eaten alive. But at least the weather is kind. It's light at four in the morning and not too cold. If she has simply run away, let's hope she sees sense soon."

It wasn't late, just gone six, so the Weavers' wasn't busy. Lily ordered a couple of pints and they sat at the bar.

"Do you want to talk about it, whatever is eating you? I don't blame you for dragging Lomax in, but he wasn't much help."

"No, it isn't just about Lomax," Matt admitted. "My mother has got herself a new boyfriend. He's a crook, but she won't listen to reason."

"All you can do is let it run its course. Fight and she'll dig her heels in. Your mother is a force when she gets going. I've met her, remember?"

Matt smiled. "You could be right. She'll probably wear him down with all her fancy ways. No one can live up to her expectations, not even me."

Chapter 21

Day 6

Matt was at his desk early the next morning, but he'd already had a text from Kate. She'd be in late again. Her brother was being discharged from hospital, and she was picking him up. He'd wanted to ask her to investigate the previous tenants of Westgate this morning, particularly the girls the neighbour had spoken about. It was too urgent to leave.

"Lily, this morning you and I will speak to Mary Salter. We're still short of information on those tenants you found out about."

"You think they can help us find Potter's killer? I've gone over all the notes, and the interviews, but I still can't spot a reason for why he had to die."

"Kate said something interesting to me on that first day. She had a theory that he was killed because of something he knew. Secrets, she said."

"In that case we need to know who he mixed with," Lily said, "anyone who had a secret worth killing for. But if there is something, it's well hidden. I've looked and looked. There is no one obvious among his small circle. And it'd have to be a pretty big secret. Given what we know about the man, it just seems a bit far-fetched."

"Mary Salter knows more about Potter than anyone. I'm convinced she's holding something back. For a start, she hasn't been truthful about those tenants. It seems to me that we have to drag every bit of useful information out of her."

"What reason would she have for holding back?" Lily asked.

"She may be covering for Potter. An empty house, a couple of young women willing to pay rent, even for a short time. Perhaps it was done without a formal agreement."

"You think they were pocketing the proceeds? Potter would know the dangers of doing that. If those girls dug their heels in, it could take months to get them out."

"Mary Salter then," Matt suggested. "Making a little money on the side. There'll be a reason she is keeping quiet."

* * *

The estate agent's office was closed, but Mary Salter was there, paperwork strewn over both desks.

"I'm trying to sort stuff out before we close," she said. "It looks like Ronald might have owed people money. There are invoices here going back months that haven't been paid."

"A neighbour told us that two young women rented the house on Westgate. You said nothing about them," Matt said.

Mary Salter looked worried. "They were desperate, the pair of them. There was no way they could have stumped up the full rent, so I let them have the house at a knockdown rate. It wasn't to be for long, just a few weeks until they got some money together. They both had jobs at some club in town. One of them, Caroline, had got herself into a bit of bother apparently."

"You said nothing about this. Why?"

"I thought it might complicate things."

"Can we have their names?" Lily asked.

"Look, I wasn't doing anything wrong. I didn't tell Ronald because he was such a stickler for agreements and the like."

"The names!" Lily reiterated.

"Amy Oliver and Caroline Perks."

Matt looked at Lily. Caleb Fletcher had spoken about a Caroline, another girl who'd gone missing from the Red Stiletto.

"Do you know a club in town called the Red Stiletto?" Lily asked her.

She sniffed. "I know of it, but I've certainly never been there. It's not my sort of place. Why? Is that where the girls worked?"

"We think so. You're sure they said they were working in a club?"

"Yes. Why is that so important?"

Matt inhaled. He hadn't said anything to Mary Salter about the find in the cellar at Westgate, but perhaps the time had come. "Potter wasn't the only body found in that house. We did a search and found bones in the cellar, a young woman's. Someone had attempted to conceal her identity by burning her."

Mary Salter turned pale. "You can't possibly think that I had anything to do with that? Or Ronald either, for that matter."

"At this time, we are not sure, Ms Salter. But now you know why it's important that you tell us everything you can about those two girls."

"I've no idea where they went. I used to see Amy regularly. It was her came into the office to pay the rent, always in cash. But I never saw the other one, Caroline."

"What was Caroline scared of?" Lily asked.

"Her husband. And before you ask, I've no idea who he is. She was terrified of him, so Amy said. According to her, he's a bad lot. Reckoned that if he caught up with Caroline, she was dead. Amy told me that the man's an animal. He wants revenge because she cheated on him."

"Name, please," Matt said.

Mary Salter shook her head. "I don't know."

"I don't believe you."

"I'm telling you the truth. Amy said it was better if I didn't know the details. She insisted, said it was safer for me. But I do know where Caroline lived before she left him. I presume you'll find her husband there. Ronald handled the sale, you see. But there were no names. The property was purchased, and is listed as belonging to a firm called 'Hilltop Investments'. The house is in Slaithwaite — Hilltop House, up on Ogden Moor."

"He's got money then," Lily observed.

"Ill-gotten gains more like," Mary Salter said. "A man that shifty, I doubt he's done a proper day's work in his entire life."

"Where is Caroline now?"

"She might still be in hiding, staying with one of the other girls from that club, but I've no idea who with or where."

"She isn't with her boyfriend?" Lily asked. "Surely the pair of them would have done a runner by now. Got well away from here."

"The man Caroline took up with is dead. It was him you pulled out of the canal the other day."

That came as a shock. Matt knew about the link between Ainley and Lomax, but that was as far as it went. Still, it made a sort of sense. The Red Stiletto did belong to Ainley, and Caroline had worked there. "Did Caroline's husband have an interest in the Red Stiletto? Or know a man called Martin Lomax?"

"I've no idea."

Mary Salter opened her mouth, then closed it again. She knew more. "What is it?" Matt asked.

"It might be nothing."

"I'll be the judge of that."

"The Red Stiletto, you said. I think Francine worked there for a while."

* * *

The data from Karen Fletcher's laptop and mobile phone had been analysed, and Kate was sitting at her desk, scanning the printouts. Kaz's browsing history was interesting. As they suspected, she had accessed the Red Stiletto website a number of times. But she'd also been researching names connected to the current case. Martin Lomax for one, and Pamela Ansel. But there was a name there that Kate didn't know — Jack Flanagan. Karen also used a number of social media platforms. Most of what she wrote was just prattle to her girlfriends. Kate ran through her list of friends. Karen Fletcher knew most of the girls from the club, including Caroline and Lisa.

It appeared that Karen had been busy. During the last fortnight she'd spoken on her phone to Pamela Ansel and, interestingly, Martin Lomax. But both Ansel and Lomax had insisted they hadn't heard from her. Why was that, Kate wondered? What were they trying to hide? There were also a number of calls to an unknown number. Kate wrote it down on her notepad.

Chapter 22

Matt called a case conference.

"Mary Salter has admitted to letting the Westgate house to two young women, Caroline Perks and Amy Oliver. Amy is the girl who left the Red Stiletto with nowhere to go, so that makes sense. Salter assures us that she has no idea where either of them is now. Caroline was having an affair with Paul Ainley — the body in the car. Like it or not, we'll have to liaise with Carlisle on this one. He could well have information that will prove useful, particularly regarding the whereabouts of Caroline Perks. Salter doesn't know what happened to Amy." He turned to Lily. "We need to know more about both of them. Addresses for family members would be helpful. We could do with photos and samples of DNA from close relatives to match against the remains from the cellar. But remember, we also have Karen Fletcher missing. The one thing they all have in common is the Red Stiletto. That will be our first port of call. Salter said Amy worked there with Caroline. Given that they lived in the Westgate house, it's possible that one of them is the body in the cellar."

"I've been going through the data from Karen Fletcher's laptop," Kate said. "She knew both those girls, they've interacted on Facebook recently. I also have Karen's phone data. She made a lot of calls, several of them to an unknown mobile number." Kate paused and checked her notes. "We can now prove that Lomax was lying when he said he didn't know Karen. They too have spoken on the phone several times during the last fortnight."

Was that enough to bring him in again? "You're sure it's his — the number Karen called?"

"I took the liberty of ringing it, sir," she said. "Lomax answered. We spoke briefly about the assault on my brother. Karen also spoke to Pamela Ansel. She's another person associated with this case who has not been altogether candid with us."

"We've yet to interview Ansel. We'll see what she says first and then confront her with the evidence."

"What about Caroline's husband, sir?" Lily asked. "We should speak to him."

"Carlisle first. Think about it. This husband — and we don't yet have a name — could be the man who killed Ainley. He certainly had a motive."

"Karen researched another name, not associated with the case as far as we know. A Jack Flanagan."

Matt stared at Kate. At first he thought she was cracking some horrible joke, but she was perfectly serious.

"He could be Caroline's husband. Would you like me to check it out?" she asked.

"No!" Mat said. A uniform sitting at the back of the room jerked his head up, he'd spoken too loudly. "I'll do that." He turned to Lily. "You get on with researching Amy and Caroline. Try to find their families. Kate, speak to Pamela Ansel. Go and see her, and if she won't cooperate, bring her in. Meanwhile, I'll speak to Carlisle, then tackle Lomax." He checked the clock on the wall. "We'll report back here before close of play."

"I'll get a statement off Caleb Fletcher too," Kate said. "He knew Karen had worked at that club. Makes me wonder what else he knows. It might be worth having another word with Francine, see what she recalls from her days at the Red Stiletto."

* * *

Matt didn't know what to make of it. Kate had left the office, so he went to her desk and picked up the printed sheets. It was plain enough. IT forensics had thoroughly searched through both the laptop and the mobile phone. Karen Fletcher had been researching Jack Flanagan. But, why? How was he mixed up in this?

"You've got that look on your face again." Lily was standing behind him.

"Jack Flanagan is the man my mother is currently dating," he said. "Hearing the name gave me a shock. For all we know, he could be our murderer."

"Want me to make some discreet enquiries, sir?"

"No, Lily. I'll do it."

He decided to update Talbot. He found him in Carlisle's office, discussing the Ainley case. Matt would try to leave the personal stuff out of the conversation, but that might prove difficult.

"Ainley was having an affair with someone called Caroline Perks. What do you know about her?"

Carlisle eyed him suspiciously. "Why so curious? Want a piece of our case, do you?"

"Not from choice, but it appears we're in whether we like it or not. Caroline Perks worked for Martin Lomax, owner of the Red Stiletto club." Matt looked at Talbot. "And she was living briefly at the house in Westgate. It's possible that she or her work mate is the body in the cellar."

"Given the handbag found in the car, she could be dead too," Carlisle said. "We know about the girlfriend. Problem is, we can't find her. If she was in that car and ended up like Ainley, she could have been thrown out of her seat and ended up drifting down to the river. It's deep down there."

"Or she could be hiding from her husband. He's a jealous one. I've been told that she was terrified of him. He has to be a candidate for Ainley's murder."

"Do you have a name?" Carlisle asked.

"I was going to ask you the same question."

Matt could see that his colleague was hesitating.

"A name has come up, but you won't like it," Talbot said at last. "Jack Flanagan."

"Were you going to tell me at some stage?" Matt was annoyed that he was having to prise this out of them.

"Didn't want you getting all riled up again," Talbot said. "I've told Frank about your problem with Flanagan."

"Have you spoken to the man?" Matt asked.

"We've no idea where he is. We can't find any trace of him. He has interests in numerous businesses, so he'll be living in a house listed as belonging to one of them."

Right now, Matt wasn't inclined to share what he knew with either of them. He wanted to speak to Flanagan first. But Carlisle was one step ahead, and that was down to Talbot.

"Your mother might be able to help," Carlisle said. "Talbot told me that Flanagan is seeing her. You understand that I will have to interview her? I hope you have no objections."

Now that he'd played his hand, Carlisle sat back with that self-satisfied look on his face that Matt couldn't stand. No doubt this is what he'd been discussing with Talbot when he'd interrupted them.

"If there was a conversation about my mother, it's me you should have spoken to," he said.

"It won't be personal," Carlisle insisted. "Flanagan will be after your mother in order to get at you. He'll want to know what we've found out about his wife, and if we know where she is. Far too sensitive, that's your problem."

Matt didn't want to listen to this, and he left them to it. Later, he'd ask Talbot to speak to his mother. If she was to be interviewed, she should be told. On the plus side, his mother would finally see what kind of man this Flanagan really was.

* * *

DC Lily Haines sat at her desk, trawling through the social media sites in a search for the missing young women. Most of them had a Facebook presence, so with luck, Amy and Caroline would be no different. They already knew from the data obtained from Karen's laptop that the two were friends online as well as in the real world. Within five minutes, she'd found Amy.

But there was little information. The last time Amy had posted anything was a fortnight ago. It was nothing special, work was becoming boring and she was looking for another job. Checking through Amy's friends' list, Lily found several people with the same surname. Family members no doubt, who were possibly sheltering her. There was no sign of Caroline.

The next few hours were spent painstakingly going through Amy's contacts. Lily rang every one, leaving messages if they weren't in. But whoever she tried, the outcome was the same. No one had seen her. One woman, an aunt who lived in Birmingham, told Lily that she'd received an odd phone call from her about ten days ago. Amy had sounded frightened and wanted to visit her. Very out of character, according to the aunt.

"I had to put her off. I'm a nurse, and I work nights. The girl would have been bored to tears. Apart from which, there's no room in my small flat. You should speak to Jodie, her sister. She's local to you. She might know something."

Jodie wasn't on Amy's friends list, but the aunt was able to give Lily her phone number. Even if the sister hadn't seen Amy, they'd be able to get a photo and a DNA sample to test against the body found in the cellar.

* * *

DS Kate Baxter planned to speak to Francine first and then Pamela Ansel. After that she'd move on to Caleb Fletcher. But Francine wasn't in. Sitting in the drive, Kate took the opportunity to ring her brother, Zane. "That mate of yours, Caleb. I need to speak to him. Do you know where he is?"

"He's not with me, if that's what you're thinking. We were going up town this afternoon but he blew me out."

"I want a statement from him about the assault at the club."

"Good luck with that, sis. He's gone all quiet. Sommat's up, but he isn't saying."

Kate saw the familiar red car pull in behind her. "Got to go. Catch you later."

She put her head out of the window. "Francine! I need a word."

Francine and the boy got out of the car. "I've got my hands full. Can't it wait?"

As sullen as ever. "No, I'm afraid not. You used to work at the Red Stiletto, I believe."

"What of it?"

"Several girls who worked there have gone missing. I wondered if you knew any of them."

"I don't remember who I met. I wasn't there for long."

"Does the name Karen Fletcher ring any bells?"

"No, nothing."

"What about Amy Oliver or Caroline Perks?"

"No. Look, it's years since I was there, and they have new girls all the time."

Fair enough, Kate supposed. The three girls had worked there recently. Given how old her son was, Francine had been out of the game for a while.

Francine stared at her. "Who told you about me being at the club anyway?" Then her face cleared, and she rolled her eyes. "That gossiping hag, I'll bet. She can't resist any chance to shove the knife in."

"Who do you mean?"

"That Salter cow. She never liked me. Well, what does she know? It was a stopgap, that's all. I needed the money. Why is my stint at the club so important? It had nothing to do with Ronald's death, or anything else."

"We'll decide what's important. In one way or another, Francine, you are connected to everyone we've interviewed in this case. You were even married to the victim at one time." Kate paused. "Your name just keeps on popping up."

"It was no big deal, me working in that club," Francine said. "And I don't know anyone there now."

But Kate still thought she was keeping something back.

Chapter 23

"Lucky beggar! Fancy having a place like this to call home."

DI Frank Carlisle and Superintendent Talbot Dyson were driving up the long approach to Brindle Hall. The hall stood, majestic, at the top of the hill, with glorious views over the surrounding countryside.

"Not been 'ere before, Frank?"

The DI shook his head.

"Missed something there. They do a lovely cream tea. Sarah does a lot of the baking herself."

"Seems a bit odd that. Brindle's mother, she's got a title. They live in a place like this. You'd think the kids'd be able to put their feet up, never mind running a café and solving crime for a living."

"No money. That's what it comes down to in the end. He didn't leave them badly off, Brindle's dad, but it was nowhere near enough to keep this little lot going. The house was falling down until the lad got the bright idea of opening the place up to the public."

"What's she like, this Lady Muck?"

"Despite the airs and graces, Evelyn is a fine woman. I can't see her knowingly doing anything against the law. This man, Flanagan, has wormed his way into her life. Matt reckons he did it deliberately, by staging a robbery that nearly came off. Flanagan turns up and sends the blighters packing. Saves the day. Matt thought it sus at the time. Given what we know now, I have to agree with him."

"Talbot!" Evelyn greeted the super with a delicate peck on the cheek. "You should have rung. You almost missed me." Her gaze moved to Carlisle. "A colleague of yours?"

"This is DI Frank Carlisle."

She held out a hand. "Matthew has spoken of you. But you've missed him, I'm afraid."

"It's you we want a word with," Talbot said. "It's about the other day, and what happened with that vase."

"I told Matthew that I didn't want a fuss. It all ended well. No one was harmed and they didn't take anything."

"That's not the point, Lady Brindle," Carlisle said. "You were lucky. It could have turned out very differently."

"This is about Jack, isn't it?"

"His name has come up in another enquiry. I'm concerned about you, Evelyn," Talbot said. "Flanagan is not who you think he is. The more we dig, the more I believe that what happened to you and Ivy was deliberate. He wanted to get to know you quickly, and make you trust him."

"Rubbish! Jack is a nice man. He's attentive, well mannered. There is no way he isn't genuine."

Talbot was surprised. Evelyn wasn't normally so gullible. As a rule, she was the first to be suspicious of any stranger. But, where Flanagan was concerned, she refused to see what was staring her in the face. "Evelyn, he's a dab hand at this. He's a crook. Worse than that, he could be in the frame for murder." Talbot saw the disbelief on her face. "I don't say this lightly. And I don't want you to repeat any of this to Flanagan, should you see him again. If you do, it might put you at risk."

"Why would he go to all that trouble? Coming here, pretending to be the hero like he did?"

She obviously wasn't buying it. "Like I said, he wanted to get close to you. He's done his homework. You wouldn't have gone out with him without a proper introduction." Talbot smiled. "This way, he gets round all that."

"So, what does he want?" she said.

"Does he ask about Matt and what he does, or his current case?"

"Now that you ask, yes. We went to York races yesterday, and he talked about little else."

"What exactly did he ask you?" Carlisle moved closer.

"He wanted to know if Matthew was working on a murder case involving a house in Marsden. And if he was looking for missing women." She shook her head. "I didn't tell him anything. I couldn't anyway, because I never have much idea about what my son is up to."

"Did he ask you to find out?" Carlisle asked.

"No, and I wouldn't pass on such information even if I knew."

"Do you know where he lives?" Talbot asked.

"No. He either sends a car, or comes here himself to pick me up."

"And he's never bumped into Matt?"

"No, but he has met Sarah. She thought he was okay. They chatted, and she told me later that she liked him." She shook her head. "Talbot, what have we done? I've behaved like an old fool, haven't I? I really believed he was the genuine article."

Talbot had known Evelyn Brindle long enough to know that he had rattled her. The look on her face said it all. "He's good. Yes, he took you in but it was well planned. Well, you know the truth now. If he contacts you again, get in touch with me at once. It's very important that we find this man. At the moment, you're our only lead."

"You are asking me to spy for you?" She hesitated. "I'm not sure I can do that. After what you've told me, the next time Jack rings I'll be making excuses not to see him."

"Probably the best way," Carlisle said. "Does he call you on your mobile?"

Evelyn nodded.

"In that case, do you mind if we look at your calls? It might help us to find him."

Evelyn Brindle sighed heavily. "Do whatever you have to, Inspector."

* * *

Late that afternoon, Martin Lomax was sitting at the bar, palming a glass of his favourite whiskey. The police had called. He was due another visit. Having police around the club wasn't good for business, it made the punters twitchy.

A deep male voice cut into his thoughts. "You don't look well, Martin. Club getting you down, is it?"

Lomax spun round. How had Flanagan, of all people, got past security at the door? They all had strict instructions. Then he understood. Towering at Flanagan's right shoulder was his favourite henchman, Connor Brant. No one was going to refuse Connor anything. He was a giant of a man. His face was expressionless. He had no smile, ever, and no small talk.

"You know why I'm here." Flanagan perched on a stool beside Lomax. "Rumour has it that she's dead, but there's no proof of that. I believe Caroline is hiding, or someone is sheltering her. What do you think, Martin?"

"I'm sure I don't know, Jack." Lomax tried a smile, but his throat was dry, his pulse was racing and the smile was unconvincing. "Surely she'd have come home by now if she could."

"No, I don't think she would. Caroline knows me too well. She knows what's in store for her. The truth is, Martin, she's nothing but a cheating slut and the minute I find her, the bitch will rue the day she crossed me!"

"Ainley is dead. If she was in that car with him . . ."

Flanagan poured himself a drink. "You're not sheltering her, are you?"

"No, Jack!" Lomax's voice shook. "Even when she worked here, I'd no idea who she was. I'd have told you straight away if I had."

Flanagan nodded. "That's what I keep telling myself. But I know you, Martin, you have an eye for the young ones. They trust you, tell you things. You're far too soft with them. I can't believe that Caroline kept what was going on between her and that rat Ainley all to herself." He turned and winked at Brant. "So, I'll ask again, Martin. Do you know where she is?"

"No . . . No. I swear." Sweat was pouring off his face. This could get ugly very quickly.

"How's that boy of yours?" Flanagan said. "Still enjoying boarding school? Harpers in Leeds, isn't it?"

Now how did Flanagan know that? Lomax hardly ever spoke about his son. The clientele they got here, it was safer that way.

Flanagan smiled. It didn't reassure Lomax any. "They grow up so quick. He must be eighteen by now. Goes out does he, round the pubs at night? He needs to be careful. Leeds has some rough areas. Anything can happen to a fresh-faced young lad who isn't streetwise."

Lomax had heard enough. "Look, Jack, I can't help you find Caroline. Have you asked the police? They found Ainley, they might be looking for anyone who might have been in that car with him."

"Tight-lipped, the police. Besides, a young woman who used to work here reckons Caroline is alive. She says you're helping her."

Lomax gulped down the rest of his whiskey. "That's a lie! You have to believe me, Jack. I'd never cross you."

Flanagan shook his head. "Sorry, Martin, but I still don't believe you. I'm severely tempted to do you some real harm, but then again, you're useful to me. You do a pretty good job with the cash, and I'm grateful. But you're not being truthful, and I can't leave that unpunished."

Lomax got slowly up from the bar stool and backed away, terrified. "Double the amount you want me to launder if you want. We've enough capacity here. I could recruit others. I know plenty of club owners who are looking to earn extra cash."

"Cut the panic, Martin, we're leaving." Flanagan nodded at Brant. "Make sure our friend here remembers this visit."

Flanagan turned to go, but he suddenly went pale and began breathing heavily. He extracted the contents of the breast pocket of his jacket, flung them onto the counter and bent over, banging on his chest and swearing under his breath. "I'll be outside in the car," he panted. "I need my medication, and I can't stand violence."

Brant watched his boss shut the door behind him, and then pulled a handgun from his pocket. Forgetting the manner of Flanagan's departure, Lomax watched him fit the silencer, resigned to die. There was nothing he could do.

Brant's face cracked. The man was actually smiling. He raised the gun and pressed it briefly between Lomax's eyes. The metal felt cold. Then he moved it down until it settled at the shoulder joint of Lomax's right arm. He pulled the trigger.

Chapter 24

Kate stalked through the women's refuge in Huddersfield, straight to Pamela Ansel's office. One of the women had tried to stop her, saying Pamela was busy, but Kate took no notice. She was determined that, faced with their evidence, Ansel would speak the truth for once.

"We now know that you spoke to Karen Fletcher on the phone in the days before she went missing, and not just once either. You told us you hadn't heard from her. Why?"

Ansel's expression revealed nothing. "Most of what we said was just a load of rubbish about how she couldn't cope. I just let her rabbit on. It probably did her good. Karen was suffering from postnatal depression."

"I don't believe you. I think she told you about the danger she was in."

Ansel snorted. "What danger? That girl loves a melodrama. She'll have run away for the attention. If she knew that you lot were rushing around like scalded cats trying to find her, she'd be thrilled to bits."

"She worked at the Red Stiletto. Did you know that?"

"Yes, she was there for a while."

"And that didn't bother you, given her age?" Kate asked.

"I'm not her mother. Kaz was short of money, so I told her where she could earn some. I've sent a number of girls there in the past. They work, they earn. For most, it sets them back on track."

"Do you know Amy Oliver or Caroline Perks? Did you send them there too?"

"Never heard of either of them."

Kate wasn't satisfied. Yes, Ansel had admitted to knowing Karen had worked at the club, but she knew more, she was positive.

"Karen, Amy and Caroline are missing, possibly in danger. I'm not asking these questions for the good of my health, Miss Ansel." Kate made no mention of the body.

"You can ask whatever you want, but I can't guarantee that I'll have the answers. I don't know those other girls, just Karen. When she does turn up, and she will — Karen always does — then ask her."

Kate was getting nowhere. Maybe Ansel was telling the truth, she just couldn't be sure. She decided to leave it for now. "We'll talk again."

Kate's next call was to the Fletcher household. It was obvious to her that Caleb was giving Zane a swerve because she was police. The lad didn't work, so he should be at home.

Christine Fletcher answered the door. This time she appeared more relaxed, and there was no infant in her arms.

"Caleb?" Kate asked.

"He's not here."

Kate heard movement on the stairs. Someone was standing on the landing. She nodded towards them. "Who is that?"

Christine gave the figure a quick glance. "He doesn't want to talk to you. He's scared witless. Has been since your brother got himself battered."

But that was at the club. They'd been making nuisances of themselves. Kate could see no reason why the lad should hide away and be afraid to talk to her.

"Let me come in, Christine. Just fetch Caleb down here. It'll be a lot simpler than me hauling him down to the station."

Resignedly, Christine turned and went to call him.

Caleb entered, looking as if he were shielding himself behind his mother. "Can't tell you owt. Things happen. Zane got beat up. Bad business, but he should learn to keep his mouth shut. It doesn't do to pick on people like that."

"People like what, Caleb? The doormen at that club?"

"They wouldn't let us in. We were asking about Kaz. I wanted in to speak to Lomax. The doormen said no and Zane kicked off. He has a temper. You should speak to him."

Two angry lads. Kate could understand why they weren't allowed in. They'd gone about it in entirely the wrong way.

"Did you find out anything about Kaz?" she asked.

"No. No need now, anyway."

That was an odd thing to say. Kate looked from the son to the mother. Christine didn't look as worn as she had the other day. She'd had a good night's sleep, and there was no sign of the infant. Suddenly it hit her.

"She's back, isn't she? You're hiding her."

* * *

The door to the Red Stiletto was locked tight. Matt banged hard with his fist but got no response.

A woman called out to him from behind. "They're closed."

He looked round. Definitely not a dancer, she was middle-aged and struggling across the road with a bucket full of cleaning materials.

"What do you want?" she asked.

Matt showed her his badge. "Martin Lomax."

"I can let you in. I clean here. I have keys for the back door."

She led the way down an alley and round to a yard at the rear of the building.

"Mr Lomax might be in his office." She pointed to the bar and put the lights on.

Matt walked through the bar area. He spotted Lomax at once, lying in a pool of blood. Matt darted forward and checked his pulse. Lomax was still alive. Matt lost no time in ringing for an ambulance. On closer inspection, he saw that Lomax had been shot in the shoulder. The flesh had been ripped to shreds and the bone was no doubt broken. The blood was still fresh, it hadn't congealed on the floor, so this attack had happened very recently.

Matt rang the station and reported the assault. He needed forensics here quickly. He called out to the cleaning woman, "Leave that! Don't touch or move anything. Lomax has been attacked. This is now a crime scene."

"Is he alive?" she asked.

"Yes, but he's unconscious. Paramedics'll be here any minute."

Right enough, he heard the sirens coming closer. Matt rang the station again and spoke to the uniformed sergeant on duty.

"I want a close watch put on Martin Lomax. He's about to be transported to hospital. Anyone visits, get their names. The minute he comes round, let me know."

"Will he be okay?" the cleaner asked.

"Yes, I think so. This wasn't meant to kill him." Matt guessed that Lomax had probably been shot as a warning.

The big question was, who had he upset enough to do this to him?

* * *

Kate was still in the Fletchers' sitting room when she got the call from Matt. He told her what had happened to Lomax.

"Kaz is frightened," Caleb was saying. "Even if she does come down, she won't speak to you."

"She had better start talking to someone." Kate turned her phone off. "This case has suddenly gone sour. The manager of the Red Stiletto has been shot."

"Is he dead?"

"No, Caleb, so it was probably a warning. Go and bring your sister down here. I need to make sure she's safe."

Karen was thin, her clothes hung loose on her skinny frame. She was very pale. She looked as if she'd been half starved for quite some time.

Kate noticed the limp and the bandages. "What happened to your hand?"

"Accident."

"Indulge me. Describe what happened."

"Look, copper, I don't grass, so don't expect much from me. Not that there's anything I can tell you anyway."

"You knew Amy Oliver and Caroline Perks. Is that where you've been, staying with them?"

Karen looked down at her hands. "After the barney at the club, Amy said I could stay with them."

"The house on Westgate?"

Karen nodded. "I'm not saying any more."

"Look, Karen, Lomax has been attacked. He's injured and he's in hospital. He was shot. Have you any idea who might have done that?"

The girl shook her dark hair.

"Are you sure? You and he are mixed up with some dangerous people. Who knows who the next target will be?"

"Is he bad?" Karen asked.

"Bad enough. We are presuming it was a warning. It would have been an easy matter to kill him. You don't want the same thing happening to you, do you? You know Lomax, you worked at that club. What did he know that made him a target?"

Karen cleared her throat. Kate could see that she was nervous, her frightened eyes darted everywhere.

"Caroline said it wasn't safe. She was terrified of something."

"Her husband? Did she worry that he'd find out about her affair with Ainley?"

"She said he'd kill her. I told her not to be so daft, but she said I didn't know him, that he'd killed people before."

"Do you know what happened to Caroline? We can't find her."

"I've no idea."

"Her husband. What's his name?"

"I don't know. Caro wouldn't say. Perks is her maiden name. None of us ever saw him, we only ever met Ainley. He stayed at the house too. They were always whispering. He got angry. He didn't want any of us there. Reckoned we were all a liability, that we'd let something slip. I got in from the club one morning, and Amy had gone, and there was no sign of Caro."

"Had she taken her things? Left you a message? Anything?"

"All her stuff was still in their room. But she had taken that red bag of hers. Never went anywhere without it."

"What happened next?"

"I got a call. Some woman wanted to know where Caroline was. She said there was money in it if I spoke to her."

That must be the cash that had been found in Karen's room.

"Did you know her?"

Karen shook her head.

"Did she have a youngish voice, or was she older?"

Karen shrugged.

"Come on, Karen. You spoke on the phone. Was it her who kept you prisoner? If so you must have met her. Who is she?"

"I'm not sure. My head's all over the place. I never saw her properly. I was drugged," Karen whined.

"Okay. What did you do when she rang?"

"I told her I wanted the money up front. She didn't want to meet me in person, so she sent it through the post to this address. I was to take Caro to her the next day. She said that if I double crossed her, there'd be trouble." Karen looked down at her hands. Blood was seeping through the dressings. "I should have listened to her."

"This woman. She must have been working for Caroline's husband, I suppose," Kate said.

"I don't know. I was supposed to take Caro to a certain house, but it was too late. Then that morning Caro did one before I got up. I'd no idea where she'd gone. I just kept hoping she'd turn up. The woman rang me. I daren't tell her, so I went to the meet alone. I thought she might give me more time."

"That was stupid. Why not call us?" Kate said.

"And say what? I didn't know how bad things would get."

"Where is this house?"

"Just some house on an estate."

Kate was getting fed up with these woolly answers."When you told her there was no Caroline, what did she do?"

"At first we talked. She seemed reasonable. I explained about Caro. I told her there were a few places I could try, and to give me a few hours more."

"She didn't agree?"

"No, she drugged me and locked me up. I spent days in a bloody cold cellar with precious little to eat. When I wouldn't talk, she did this." Karen held up her hands. "She ripped the nails off some of my fingers, cruel bitch!"

Kate winced. "Who is this woman? You met her. You must be able to describe her. And where is the house? I want answers, Karen. Refuse to cooperate and I'll take you down to the station."

The girl wasn't listening. Her phone had just beeped and she was intent on the screen. "Sorry, that's all you're getting. I daren't say any more."

"What is it, Karen? Has someone just threatened you?"

"Mind your own business," Karen said.

Kate reached forward and snatched the mobile from Karen's grasp. The words she read sent an icy shiver down her spine.

Talk and your kid won't live out the week.

Chapter 25

It had been a long, exhausting day, but there was still a lot to organise before anyone went home. Matt had gathered the team together in the incident room.

"We have put a twenty-four-hour watch on Martin Lomax, and Karen Fletcher and her family," he told them. "As you know, Lomax was shot this afternoon and a threat was made against Karen's child."

"Karen knows who held her captive and the location. She would have told me, I feel sure of that, but then she got that text and clammed up," Kate said.

"They threatened her child," Lily reminded her. "That would make anyone think twice."

"Nonetheless, if we are to help her we need to know who she is afraid of," Matt said. "Speak to her again tomorrow. Assure her that we'll keep her safe. We can put the family into witness protection if need be."

"I'll try, sir, but after what she's been through, the girl is genuinely frightened. I'm sure she knows who held her captive and butchered her fingers, but she won't say. That's a measure of how terrified she is."

"Someone is desperate to find Caroline Perks. It strikes me that they'll go to any lengths. She was having an affair with Paul Ainley. He's dead, but we've found no trace of her. We have no proof that she's alive either, but whoever is looking for her appears to think she is. Caroline worked at the Red Stiletto. She knew Lomax, and Karen too. She and Karen lived under the same roof for a while."

"I had a look at the incident board for the Ainley case," Kate said. "A red handbag was found in the boot of that car. Caroline had one and she took it everywhere, so I've been told. If she was in that car, I don't think much of her chances."

"Any joy with finding Caroline's relatives?" Matt asked Lily.

"Not yet, sir, but the sample for Jodie Oliver is in the lab," Lily said. "And we now have a photo. I've put it on the incident board."

"With any luck we should know tomorrow whether Amy is our body in the cellar."

"Whoever she is, we still don't have a motive, or a suspect," Lily said.

"Potter was killed, Ainley too, and a young woman. There has to be something connecting them. Do we have anyone in the frame?" Kate asked.

"Caroline's husband is favourite," Lily said. "Jealousy being the motive for the Ainley killing. If he found out about the Westgate house, he could have gone there. Potter got in the way and was killed too."

"Do we have a name for this husband?" Kate asked.

Matt didn't reply. He'd yet to visit the house up on Ogden Moor that was owned by one of Jack Flanagan's companies. "Do a search of the marriage registers," he said to Lily. "See if you can find an entry for Caroline Perks. And not a word to anyone." He didn't write this one on the board. He wanted to get to Flanagan before Carlisle. "Make it urgent. First thing tomorrow."

It was nearly nine. They should be going home.

"I'll stay, and do it now," Lily said. "I've nothing on."

"Are you sure?" She nodded. "If you get anything, text me. I'll be at the hospital."

"You think Lomax will talk to you?" Kate asked doubtfully.

"His life could depend on it."

* * *

Martin Lomax had had an operation to stem the blood loss, and they had attempted to repair the damage to his shoulder and upper arm. The bullet had torn into the muscle, sinew and bone, wreaking havoc. The surgeons were pleased with the outcome, but they couldn't promise that he'd get full use back.

Lomax had had a hefty dose of morphine and was comfortable for the time being. But he was tormented by memories of what had happened to him. Flanagan was a ruthless man. He would stop at nothing to find his wife. The pain, the horror of what Connor Brant had done bounced around in Lomax's mind. He could easily have been killed. If there was one thing Lomax had learned from the experience, it was that he needed a way out. Working at the club brought him into constant contact with Flanagan's people. Flanagan laundered money through his club, and many others. He'd been doing it for years. The current stash of money was rumoured to be from cash in transit between two banks in Leeds. The work was easy and lucrative. Lomax got a percentage of everything he put through the till.

As he regained consciousness, Lomax became aware of his mobile constantly beeping. The text messages were coming in thick and fast, and they all said the same thing. Speak to the police and he'd be pushing his son around in a wheelchair for the rest of his life. Given what he'd just been through himself, Lomax had no reason to doubt that Flanagan meant it.

He spotted Matt Brindle talking to a nurse in the corridor. Damn the man. All Lomax wanted was to be left alone.

The detective entered the room where Lomax lay. "You were lucky. That was close. Do you know who attacked you?"

Lomax shook his head. "No idea. He was wearing a mask. It was a robbery gone wrong. He made a grab for the till and I got in the way."

"Not Flanagan looking for his errant wife?"

"I've no idea who you're talking about."

Matt sat down beside the bed. "I think you have. You knew Paul Ainley, you worked for him. He ran off with Flanagan's wife, who worked at your club for a while. It was the obvious place for the villain to look. It's about time you realised the danger you're in. Flanagan won't be content with lies. You can't fob him off. You know more than you've told me, no doubt more than you told him. If you want to survive, then you need us, Lomax."

"Like I said, a robbery gone wrong. I can't help you. I've no idea who he was."

"Does Flanagan have something on you? Have you been threatened, or a family member perhaps?"

"I don't have any family," Lomax lied.

"We can protect you. There'll be an officer just out there at all times."

Lomax laughed. He could imagine how Brant'd deal with anyone who got in his way, police or not.

"Do one, copper. I don't need your help. Nothing happened that you can do anything about."

"I don't believe you. You need to trust us, Lomax. But we'll set that aside for the time being. You lied to me about Karen Fletcher. You do know her. We have your phone data, and we know the pair of you talked. Care to tell me what about?"

Lomax shook his head. His shoulder was starting to hurt again. He didn't need the third degree. "Young women, you know what they're like. Wanting time off, wanting to change their hours. It was never anything important."

"Why not simply tell us you knew her when we asked?"

"Look, copper, I didn't know what she'd want me to say. I'm not their bloody keeper. Best not get involved, that's my motto."

"I'm afraid you are involved now, Mr Lomax. I'll leave you my card just in case. Anytime you want to tell me what really happened, just ring."

Chapter 26

Day 7

Matt Brindle woke late. His mother had called him but he'd turned over and gone back to sleep.

"You're working too hard," she said, when he finally walked into the kitchen. "Ivy has done you a couple of poached eggs, and there's tea in the pot."

"I don't want you to see Flanagan again, Ma."

"I know you don't." She gave a humourless laugh. "Set the heavy mob on me, didn't you, son? I had Talbot and friend round here. They don't like him much either."

"He's a suspect in a murder investigation, and possibly a severe wounding as well."

"They didn't tell me the details but they made it clear enough."

"Just do as I ask you. If he rings, make an excuse."

Matt didn't feel like eating. He poured himself a large mug of tea and went into the main hall. The house wasn't open yet, but it was another sunny day so they'd be busy.

His mobile rang. It was Lily.

"I've found Caroline's mother, sir," she said. "She lives in Halifax. I'm on my way there now. I'll get a DNA sample and a photo. Do I tell her what's going on?"

"We have no idea ourselves, do we? For now, just tell her Caroline is missing. Ask if she knows anything about that husband of hers. A photo of the wedding would be useful. What about the results of the DNA sample from Jodie Oliver?"

"The lab says later today. By the way, I found that information you wanted last night. I didn't text because I wasn't sure it was correct. I've left a note on your desk. Caroline did marry, but it's odd—"

At that point, Matt lost her. She must have been up in the hills where the signal was bad. They'd speak again later.

Matt had already decided that he'd venture up to Ogden Moor this morning, and talk to Flanagan. He should ring Kate, let her know he'd be late. But his mobile rang again. It was Talbot.

"Get yourself in here," Talbot said without preliminaries. "No detours, now. We need to talk, and it's urgent."

* * *

Kate was getting ready for work. "Have you spoken to Caleb Fletcher since yesterday?" she asked Zane.

"Doesn't want to know, does he? Which is a right shame, sis, because I thought we were doing fine."

"Contact him. Go round and see him today. See if you can find out if he knows anything about Karen. Where she's been, who held her captive."

"You've got them under police guard! He won't want to talk to me now."

"Just try, Zane. Kaz knows a lot more than she's saying, and it could help us catch a murderer."

"Are you going to see her?"

"Perhaps, but later. If you get anything, ring me."

Kate left for the station. As she drove, she tried to piece together what they had. Two dead males. Ainley, she could understand. He had upset Caroline's husband and from all accounts, he was a thug. But what had Ronald Potter done to upset someone that much? Another conversation with Mary Salter might throw some light. They now had names that they hadn't put to her before.

Kate pulled into the car park on Marsden High Street and rang the station. She told one of the uniforms in the main office what she was up to and to leave a note on Matt's desk.

Kate entered the office to find Julie seated at Mary Salter's desk. "Not shut up shop yet?"

Julie looked up at her. "Too much paperwork. We have sales going through, and the solicitors are asking for stuff. With luck it will quieten down by the end of the week. We'll close then."

"Is Ms Salter in?"

"It's her break. She shouldn't be long. I think she's gone to do a bit of shopping. Can I help?"

"Did Mr Potter ever talk about someone called Paul Ainley?"

The young woman keyed the name into their database. "I don't recall the man, but he did rent a property from us. There are some notes on the record that Ronald made. It says here that Ainley insisted on the transaction being kept secret. According to this, the cottage was all about getting peace and quiet." She looked up at Kate. "A little unconventional, but Ronald must have been okay with it."

"Has anyone else asked you about Ainley?"

"You'd have to ask Mary, but I don't think so."

Kate thought about this for a moment. "This cottage, was it his main address?"

"No. He owns a property in Huddersfield. That's where he is listed as living according to the electoral roll."

"The address, please. Do you have a spare set of keys for the cottage?"

"It's up Hade Edge. Drive through the village and take the first track on your right. It's the small stone cottage after the farm with the green paintwork. You can't miss it. Calder Beck runs right past the back garden and down the hill." She scribbled the postcode on a scrap of paper and handed it to Kate with a set of keys.

Back in her car, Kate got out her map of the area. Hade Edge was a tiny village consisting of only half a dozen dwellings, up in the hills near Holmfirth. She punched the postcode into her satnav and was off.

The drive took her through a number of pretty Pennine villages, all of which had a row of stone cottages bordering the main roads. At this time of year, the walls of those cottages were festooned with climbing plants, clematis and honeysuckle. But Kate was a realist. Come winter, this place would be well-nigh impassable, cut off by snow and ice. The countryside was all very well, but would she ever get the city out of her soul?

After a few false turns, she finally found the track Julie had told her about. She drove on, and about half a mile past the farm she saw the cottage. Well, for someone wanting peace and quiet, this was the place alright.

The cottage looked deserted. There were no vehicles in the driveway and all the blinds were shut. Kate alighted from her car and knocked on the door. There was no answer. She cupped a hand against the front window, and peered inside. She could see nothing.

Then she heard footsteps. There was someone inside. The front door opened a crack, and a pair of terrified eyes stared back at her. It was a woman.

"Who are you?"

"Police. DS Kate Baxter, East Pennine CID. And you?"

"Caroline Perks."

Kate heaved a sigh of relief. "We thought you were dead. Your boyfriend has been murdered, and no one has seen you for days. Why didn't you tell someone where you were?"

"You'd better come in."

At the very least, Kate was expecting an explanation of some sort. What she got came completely out of the blue. She'd no sooner set foot in the hallway than a blow to the back of her head knocked her to the floor, unconscious.

Chapter 27

"Why the summons, Talbot? What's so urgent it can't wait?"

Talbot Dyson was sitting behind his desk, looking uncomfortable. "You won't like it."

"What is it? Something I've done? Something my mother's done?"

"No. It's this man, Jack Flanagan. I want you to drop it as of now."

Matt was flabbergasted. "He's our prime suspect in a murder case! The missing girls — remember them? Plus, the shooting at the club yesterday. Then there is Ainley. No one had a better motive than Flanagan for killing him."

"That's Carlisle's case, or have you forgotten?"

Matt watched Talbot shift in his seat. He wasn't happy. "Are you going to tell me why?"

"It's out of my hands. I reckon that before long, the Flanagan case will be given to another team entirely."

Now Matt was intrigued. Talbot must have been told something and been instructed not to talk about it. The look on the super's face said it all. He'd been given no choice.

"If it was up to me, I'd let you in, but I have my orders," he said.

"What team?" Matt asked. "Surely you can tell me that."

"Regional Crime Squad."

"What's Flanagan done to attract their interest?"

"I can't say any more. I have my orders too, lad."

"Something serious then. Flanagan is up to something big, more far reaching than what happened to Ainley, not that that wasn't bad enough."

"It would seem so," Talbot said. "But that's all you're getting. Back to work, and leave this one alone."

For now, Matt would have to accept this whether he liked it or not. He went back to the incident room. No Kate, and no Lily, but there were a couple of notes on his desk. One from Kate, explaining that she'd gone to speak to Mary Salter again. No doubt to tie up a couple of loose ends. He wasn't really interested. All he could think of was Flanagan. Matt was angry and frustrated that he couldn't go after this man.

The note from Lily was just a few words in her usual scrawl. She'd investigated Caroline's marriage, and found what they needed. But what she had written on the note shook him to the very core.

He'd taken it for granted that the entry at the registry office would show that Caroline had married Jack Flanagan. But that wasn't the case. He sat down and read the note again. The man Caroline Perks had in fact married was Jack Waddell!

Jack Waddell. The one name that had the power to terrify Matt, and keep him awake nights.

Waddell was a villain who for years had kept one step ahead of the law. He was known to be behind most of the organised crime in this area and beyond. Despite many investigations, a team in Leeds had never managed to get sufficient proof to nail him. Witnesses disappeared, others had accidents and even more clammed up. Waddell had a long reach and even when he was out of the area, he terrified anyone involved with him.

The name had haunted Matt since the day he'd first heard it. A few months ago, he'd been given information by a prisoner he'd interviewed as part of another investigation. That man had said that Jack Waddell was behind what had happened to him and DS Paula Wright on that fateful day. He'd insisted that it was down to Waddell that Paula was dead and Matt badly injured.

At the time, Matt had discussed it with Talbot, but as far as he knew it hadn't been taken any further. Matt stared at the words, hardly able to believe what he was reading. How could this be? The fear, the panic that grabbed him periodically was back with a vengeance. He felt as if the room was closing in around him. He closed his eyes and was back in that stone building, high in the hills. He saw Paula, standing by the broken window, calling to him. Matt felt as if someone had kicked him in the guts. He was momentarily paralysed. He couldn't even speak.

He hated feeling like this. Hated the fact that Waddell had the power to turn his world upside down. Seeing that man's name had brought on a full-blown panic attack. Matt knew he had to shake himself, get it together. One way or another, he had to put a stop to Waddell for good.

Matt accessed the police database. Jack Flanagan had to be an alias used by Waddell. Talbot knew, and that's why he wouldn't talk. But whether Talbot talked or not, Matt had to find out what was known about that day.

The record was locked.

Matt was shaking. The man had been seeing his mother! His only reason had to be to get access to him. But what did he want? It could only be to find out where Caroline was.

Matt shook himself. He needed to know what information Talbot had. This was no time for secrets. Waddell was wandering the streets of their patch, doing whatever he pleased. People were dead, a man had been shot and a young woman scared witless. Seconds later, he was back in Talbot's office.

"Don't lie to me, Talbot. Not about this. Flanagan is really Waddell, isn't he? What exactly do you know?"

The super sighed heavily. "It was the fingerprints. They were a perfect match to what we have on record."

"You know where Flanagan really is. Let me bring him in. Interview him about that day and what he did."

"No. That would be stupid. It will jeopardise the entire operation. You were a target, you have to keep away."

"You do accept that Waddell was responsible for what happened to me and Paula that day?"

"Yes. We take the murder of one of our own very seriously," Talbot said acidly. "That's why you mustn't go near him. There is a team from Leeds assigned to the case. They have received some intel which suggests that the ambush was down to Waddell. The fact he is around here masquerading as Flanagan is purely down to his search for his wife. A lucky break for us, because it has finally flushed him out. It was the fingerprints on the Moorcroft that did it. Bit of good work that."

"You know who the young scallies are too?"

"Yes, and they are being rounded up as we speak."

"What about the two cases? Carlisle wants Waddell for suspected murder, and I want to speak to him about the girls. Not to mention the shooting incident at the club."

"Once he has been apprehended, a member of your team will be allowed to interview him. But strictly on the understanding that they do not get into a screaming match about you or Paula."

"When is he being arrested?"

"He is holed up in a house on Ogden Moor. He'll be taken to the station in Leeds and interviewed there."

* * *

Barbara Perks lived on the outskirts of Halifax. The house was pleasant enough, a stone terrace in a neat side street.

Lily had rung her in advance and was expected. "I'm here about Caroline," Lily said. "Can you tell me when you last saw her?"

Barbara Perks looked concerned. She invited Lily inside, and they sat down to talk. "I haven't seen her recently," she said. "To be frank, I can't stand that man she's married to. I can't imagine what possessed her. She's a pretty girl, and he's twice her age. The money he flashes about must have turned her head. Nothing else makes any sense."

"She doesn't visit? You don't meet in town, go shopping?"

"I haven't seen her since Christmas. She came one afternoon, had some tea, we swapped presents and that was that."

"And there's been nothing since?"

"The odd call. He doesn't approve of her going out alone, you see. Ever since they first met, he's kept Caroline under his thumb. Is she in trouble?"

What to tell her? "I'm not sure, Mrs Perks. As far as we know, Caroline is missing. No one has seen her in a while."

"But you do think she's okay? I mean, nothing has happened to her, has it? I know we're a bit distant at the moment, but I expect that'll change in time. She'll see sense. I know my Caroline, she will come home eventually."

"We hope so." Lily tried on a reassuring smile.

"You don't look too sure. You know something, don't you? You're worried that something's happened to her, that he's done something to her!"

"We just don't know, Mrs Perks. Officially, she is missing."

Barbara Perks's face crumpled and she looked close to tears. "You have to find her, bring her home."

"We think Caroline might be hiding, possibly from her husband." Lily added in an effort to comfort her. "What I want is a photo and a DNA sample from you. That way, if we find any young women who are reluctant to tell us who they are, we can do tests."

"He did this. He made her run away. He's an evil man. I tried to tell her, but at the beginning she was besotted with him and wouldn't listen."

"You said at the beginning," Lily noted. "Did things change?"

"I'm not sure. When she was here at Christmas, I got the feeling she was trying to tell me something. She looked different, happier. I did wonder if she'd found someone else. That could be where she's gone, off with her new man."

Lily suspected that someone else was Paul Ainley. "The tests will be quick, Mrs Perks, and I'll let you know straight away if we find a match."

Back in her car, Lily rang the station, to find out if anything had happened in her absence. The uniformed officer manning the office phone told her that they were all out. But he did have a message for her. The bank had been in touch. The notes found in Karen Fletcher's bedroom were part of a robbery haul from two years ago. A vehicle transporting cash from one bank to another had been attacked on a country road outside Skipton, not far from Leeds. The robbery was so well organised that the police suspected that inside information had been acquired. Tens of thousands were taken and none of it had ever been recovered. They also retrieved fingerprints from the plastic bags, but they weren't on file.

Lily sat in her car for a few minutes and thought about this. What was Karen Fletcher doing with cash from the haul? And more importantly, who had given it to her? She'd told them it was payment for handing Caroline over.

Lily grabbed her phone and texted Matt. This was too important to leave until she got back to the station.

Chapter 28

"We'll be getting out of here shortly, Brant, and I don't want to leave any loose ends."

The big man grunted. "What about the wife?"

"Caroline will come out of hiding sooner or later. When she does, there are enough people in this town who'll tell me. After what happened to Lomax, no one will dare shelter her. Besides, I need a rest. Tearing around Yorkshire trying to find her isn't doing me any good. I saw the quack yesterday, he's upped my pills." He tapped his chest. "The old ticker won't last much longer unless I take it easy."

"Want me to prime a few faces? Perhaps a reward would encourage a response."

"You know, Brant, there are times when I see exactly why I took you on. Do that. Ten grand to whoever delivers the bitch to the Red Stiletto."

The big man nodded.

"Lomax is still in hospital. Visit him. Ensure that he's under no illusions about what is required. I want him to know that his son's continued safety depends on his silence. He talks about our business once we've left, and they'll both regret it. And tell him to shift himself. I want him back at work, pronto."

Brant left to get ready.

Waddell, the man they called Flanagan, picked up his phone and made a call. He periodically rang his wife's mobile, though he didn't expect a reply.

"I'm leaving now," Brant was saying. "The hospital first and then where, boss?"

"Do a round of the clubs. Make sure they understand what I want from them. We'll have another load of cash to clean up by the end of the week. I want things moving."

"What about the Red Stiletto?"

"I'm putting another manager in for the time being. It's all been sorted with Ainley's sister. She trusts my judgement." He smiled. "It'll be someone I can trust and who knows the business. And who'll deliver Caroline to me if someone finds her." He smiled icily at Brant. "Thomas from Belfast will do the job. No one in their right mind would cross him. That should make for a quiet life."

Brant left, and Waddell's mobile rang. When he saw the number, he frowned. "What now?"

"I can help. I know what you want and I can get it for you."

"I'll have what I want soon enough. I have no more need of you. You let me down once. You don't get a second chance."

"Pity. I'm looking at her now. What do I do, set her free to go to the police? I will, you know, but I thought I'd give you first option."

"Okay, the deal stands. You know where, and don't let me down this time."

* * *

Connor Brant had been with Waddell for years. As a rule, he had little involvement in his boss's business. He did as he was told without asking questions, and their relationship was thus hassle free, and Waddell paid well. But for the past two years, Brant had had a complication in his life that Waddell was unaware of. He had a woman.

Waddell's search for his wife had come to an end for the time being. Another job was being planned, several hundred miles from here. Brant knew that Waddell would want him there to oversee things, but that would take him away from this area, and from his lady. They had had a couple of years of relative freedom. Waddell wasn't in the least bit interested in Brant's private life. The big man was seriously debating whether or not to split with the villain. It wasn't something he had ever considered doing before.

Once he was alone, Brant rang her on his mobile. He needed to see her. "Things are set to change, Babe," he growled. "I'll be leaving at a moment's notice. No time for long goodbyes, I'm afraid."

"You can't do that, Con! Things still need clearing up. The police are all over the Potter killing, and the missing girls. What if there are more questions? I need you close."

"That'll take a while. Trust me. The police are idiots."

"Con, I don't want you to go. We made plans."

He heard the pain in her voice. This wasn't what either of them wanted, and it was down to Waddell. "There is a way round it, but it'll mean ditching the boss. That'll be risky. I know things. He'll consider me a risk and want me dead. He'll put a price on my head. If we go, it will have to be quick, and we can't let anyone find out."

"Just tell me when and where, that's all I need."

Her voice quivered with emotion. She sounded so sure. For the first time in his life, Connor Brant had found a woman who loved him.

"Pack a few things. I'll be in touch."

* * *

Matt wanted another word with Lomax. The short hop from the station to the hospital gave him some time to think. He had no choice but to do as Talbot wanted, but that didn't stop him questioning others who might be connected to Waddell. And high on the list was Lomax. Waddell had a problem with Ainley and he owned the Red Stiletto. Waddell would know by now that Caroline had worked in the club, and he too would have questions. That could well be what the shooting was all about. Lomax denied knowing Waddell, but there had to be a link. Matt was certain that the villain had gone to that club and shot Lomax.

As he pulled into the car park, his mobile beeped. It was the text from Lily, telling him that the cash they'd found in Karen's room was part of a bank heist. No one had been brought to book and to date this was the only cash that had turned up.

Someone looking for Caroline had access to that money. Did that mean that the robbery was down to Waddell? Matt made his way up to the ward, thinking it over.

Lomax was on his own in a small room just off the main ward.

"How are you doing?" Matt asked.

"No better for seeing you. What do you want now?"

"Tell me about your relationship with Flanagan — or should I call him Waddell?"

At the sound of that name, Lomax turned pale. "I don't know any Flanagan, or any Waddell. You've got me mixed up with someone else."

Ignoring his protestations, Matt said, "Did he come to the club? Did you ever see him meet with Ainley?"

"You've got it all wrong. I can't help you."

Matt was standing with his back to the door and didn't hear the footsteps behind him. Until Brant coughed.

"This man bothering you, Mr Lomax?"

Matt spun round and stared into a pair of cold, dark eyes. He'd no idea who this man was, but he obviously wasn't someone you got on the wrong side of. He was huge, and in first class shape. This one worked out, and would no doubt pack quite a punch.

"And you are?" Matt asked.

"None of your business."

"That's where you're wrong." Matt showed Brant his warrant card. "Who are you, and what do you want with Lomax?"

"A word. Club business. Now do one, copper. This has nothing to do with you."

Matt glanced at Lomax and saw that he was quaking in terror. "Sorry, I'm not going anywhere."

Brant's eyes narrowed and his mouth drew into a thin line. He wasn't used to folk giving it back. All of a sudden, he emitted a loud roar, pulled himself to his full height, grabbed Matt under both arms and lifted him bodily from the room. He threw him unceremoniously down on the corridor floor, and slammed the door shut behind him.

This was no time for wounded pride. Matt took his mobile and rang the station. He wanted backup, now.

Brant had pushed a chair up beneath the door handle, jamming it shut. Helpless, Matt watched through the window. Brant had Lomax by the throat and was shouting at him. Matt had never seen him before, and guessed that he was one of Waddell's men.

Backup soon arrived, and they used an enforcer to ram the door open. After a scuffle, Brant was handcuffed and led away, shouting back to Lomax.

"If I was you, I'd ring that boy of yours and say goodbye!"

When Matt went back into the room, Lomax yelled at him, "Look what you've done! What chance does Jason have now? The bastard has threatened to put him in a wheelchair!"

"Jason is your son?" Matt had wondered if there was someone Lomax was afraid for. "Where is he? We'll give him protection, you too."

"You're a bloody fool! Do you think it's that easy to get the better of Waddell?" Lomax sneered.

"So you do know him?" Matt said.

"You'll never get me to admit that on the record."

"It was him shot you in the club."

"I don't know the man, and he's never been to the club," Lomax said.

"That man who was just here, who is he?"

"A brute called Connor Brant."

"He works for Waddell?" Matt asked.

"If he does, Waddell will have him out before the day is done."

"I seriously doubt that. He assaulted you, and I witnessed it," Matt said.

"Don't waste your time, I won't report it. Nothing happened — got it?"

"Even if you stay silent, there's no guarantee that your son will be safe. You need us for that, Lomax."

Lomax turned his face to the wall. "Get lost. I've nothing to say."

Matt looked down at him. The wound in his shoulder was bleeding again. He wasn't getting out of here anytime soon. "The offer still stands. Decide you do need help, you ring me."

* * *

When Matt returned to the station, Lily was back.

She grinned at him. "You've had a bit of excitement, I hear."

"The man's an animal. What have they done with him?"

"He's in a cell. Causing quite a stir, apparently. His name is Connor Brant. Someone from Leeds is coming to collect him." She looked at Matt. "Is there something I should know?"

Matt shook his head. "I don't know all the answers myself. I'm presuming Brant works for Waddell."

"Waddell, as in Caroline's husband?"

"Flanagan is an alias Waddell uses," Matt said. "They're one and the same person. And the powers that be have warned me off. Waddell is the man who killed Paula and injured me. At least, one of his minions did." He thought for a moment. "For all we know, it could have been that brute in the cells."

"Now I'm confused. Flanagan is really Waddell, who's wanted for what happened to you and your sergeant. But we want him because of the Ainley killing and the missing girls. Is that about right?"

"Talbot has promised that one of us will get to interview Waddell. By now, the Leeds lot should have arrested him and put him in a cell."

Lily sniffed. "I'm not surprised Caroline went off him. By the way, I've dropped off the saliva sample from her mother at the lab. We should know very soon if the body in the cellar is Amy or Caroline."

"But will that actually help?" Matt stared at the incident board. "If it is Caroline, it makes some sort of sense. Waddell finally caught up with her and took his revenge. But then, why has he been searching for her so hard these last few days? If it's Amy, what had she done to deserve being killed?"

"And don't forget Potter. It was him who got us into this, remember? What did he do to attract Waddell's attention?"

Matt had no answer for this. "Have you heard from Kate?"

"Nothing. I tried her mobile just before you got back, but it was dead. I'm presuming she's got no signal, wherever she's gone off to."

Matt shook his head. "She went to see Mary Salter in Marsden."

Chapter 29

Kate drifted in and out of consciousness. Try as she might to shift the fog, her head just wouldn't clear. Each time her eyes fluttered open, she tried to make sense of her surroundings. She was in a damp, dark room with the merest chink of light peeping through a boarded up window. She could just make out the pattern on the wallpaper. It was several decades old. Kate recalled her granny having something similar in her bedroom.

Her head ached. Feeling around it tentatively, she found a sore lump at the back, and there were dark smudges on her fingers — blood. Someone must have hit her. She tried to remember.

Kate found that she was lying on the floor. She had to at least try to sit up. Her memory was gradually returning. She'd come here looking for someone — Caroline, the missing girl. She'd found her too. It had been Caroline who'd opened the door and let her in. Kate pictured her huge, frightened eyes. But who had hit her?

Kate had to get out of here and tell the team about Caroline. They'd be wondering where she was by now. She struggled to her feet. Unsteadily, she felt her way around the walls until she found the door. It was locked. Kate pulled on the handle and cried out for help. Silence. No one was coming. No movement. Whoever had been here had left, and she was alone. Kate felt in her jacket pocket — no phone. They must have taken it. She could do nothing. With luck, Lily or the DI would read her note and ask Julie at the estate agents about the visit, then she'd send them up here.

With her back to the door, Kate slid down onto the floor. She felt dizzy and sick — concussion probably. She closed her eyes. This didn't feel real somehow, more like part of some horrible nightmare. The only hope she had left was rescue. Now she understood how that poor girl whose body they'd found must have felt.

* * *

"I tell you anything, you'll just tell that copper sister of yours," Karen grumbled.

"Kate reckons you're in danger. The man she's after is a nutter. What d'you think you're going to do if he comes looking?" Zane and Celeb were facing Karen, who was sitting on the sofa with the baby in her arms.

"There's no reason he should. I know nowt." Karen shrugged.

"But you do. You must know who kept you locked up. You told Caleb that she tried to fix your hands, so you must have seen her," Zane said.

Karen glared at him. "She fixed them alright. I'm on pills for a bloody infection, thanks to her."

"Come on, Kaz. Who was it?"

Karen Fletcher considered this.

"I've got this one to think about. They're hard nuts, these people. They won't hold back just because he's a baby. We'd both catch a bullet."

"The police are on your side," Zane said. "They'll look after you."

"That's what you say, but when it comes down to it, I'll be on my own. I always am."

Christine Fletcher tutted. "You'll have to speak to the police anyway. What about that money they found in your room?"

"I earned that. They've no right to take it." Karen handed the infant to her mother.

"How *did* you earn it, Kaz?" asked Caleb.

She shrugged. "Like I said to that detective, it was for telling the woman where Caroline was. But it all went wrong, didn't it?"

"If I get Kate to show you some photos, will you try and identify the woman who locked you up?" Zane said.

"I don't know yet. I'll think about it."

"C'mon, Kaz," Caleb said. "We don't want you getting hurt. This lot mean business. Is there anything you can tell us?"

Zane watched Karen fiddle with the dressings on her hands. He tried to fathom what might be going through her mind, but it was impossible to make out.

"You can't keep quiet. That one's safety is at stake." Caleb nodded at her son. "Tell us, Kaz. Who did that to you?"

She sighed. "Ansel, that's who it was."

* * *

Julie Powell was outside the office, just about to lock up, when Matt called out to her. "My sergeant — where did you send her?"

"She asked about a client Mr Potter dealt with. I gave her the address of a cottage he rented."

"And that's where she went?" Matt asked.

"I expect so. Why not ring and ask her?"

Matt didn't know what to think. Kate had family problems. She'd taken time off to see to her mother and been late because of Zane. Was she trying to snatch the odd hour on the side?

"This client. Was it Paul Ainley?" Matt asked.

She nodded. "That's him. The bloke they pulled out of the canal the other day."

"When was this?"

"Hours ago, but it's easy to get lost up there, even if you have good directions."

"Okay, give me the address and I'll go look for her," Matt said.

"There won't be anyone in the cottage now in any case. Mary was going to contact Mr Ainley's family to come and clear it out."

"As far as you know, was he living there alone?" Lily asked.

"That was the whole point," Julie said. "He wanted peace and quiet."

Matt and Lily returned to the car, and Lily looked at the address Julie'd given them. "It's a long way out, back of beyond and then some." Lily pulled out onto the High Street.

"Let's get there as quick as we can. Like you say, a lonely cottage. Just the place to hide away in. Who knows what Kate stumbled on?"

Chapter 30

Jack Waddell sat in an interview room with his solicitor, discussing the charges made against him.

"Murder, Charles?" Waddell was saying. "They have to be joking. What have they got exactly?"

"Last year, a detective sergeant belonging to the East Pennine force was killed, blown up. Her boss, a DI, was seriously injured in the attack."

"Attack?" Waddell laughed. "What sort of attack?"

"They were given some false information, and went out to an empty dilapidated building up in the hills. Someone threw a grenade through a gap in the stone wall. A small, confined space . . . need I say more?"

"Neat idea. One of them survived, you say. Pity." Waddell smiled evilly. "But it can't have been me. I was lying on a beach in Bali the entire month. You can ask Caroline, if she ever turns up. Even if she doesn't, there is plenty of evidence to support my alibi. Air tickets. The hotel. It's rock solid."

"They have had intelligence to back up your arrest. Someone is prepared to give evidence, Jack. I can only presume it's one of your own. You have to take this seriously. The squad here in Leeds is determined to make sure that you go down this time."

"Rubbish. There's nothing they can do. I wasn't even in the country, so how can it have had anything to do with me?"

"We are dealing with the serious crime squad, Jack. They're not your average Mr Plod. They'll have made sure of the facts before arresting you."

"They won't get anyone to stand up in court and testify against me, Charles. No one would dare. Everyone knows what happens if they do." He picked up a sheaf of papers from the table in front of them. "Now, deal with this garbage and get me out of here."

"There's more, I'm afraid. Once the people here have interviewed you, you are to be seen by detectives from the East Pennine force about another matter."

"One murder not enough for them? Jesus! What other shit are they going to throw at me?"

"The murders of Paul Ainley and Amy Oliver."

Waddell laughed out loud. "They think I killed Ainley?" He shook his head. "I wish I had, but they're clutching at straws. And who the hell is Amy Oliver?"

"What was left of her body was found in the cellar of a house in Marsden. And then of course there is the matter of the estate agent, Ronald Potter."

Waddell chuckled. "Have they lost their heads? A girl I've never heard of and an estate agent. They're having a laugh! Except that none of it is very funny." Suddenly, Waddell groaned and rubbed at his chest. He looked pale. "Bloody pain. Pass me that water, I need one of my pills. Charles, I have to get out of here before they have to carry me out in a box."

"These are serious charges, Jack, and certainly no laughing matter."

"Okay, I take your point." He took a few deep breaths. "Ah, that's better. Now, I want you to do something for me, Charles." He looked around, saw no cameras. They were alone in the room. "No questions, and you don't tell a soul."

"You know me, Jack. Anything to help."

Waddell snorted. "I know that I pay you well enough. All you have to do is ring this number. When they answer, you say just two words. Just two. Got it?" Jack Waddell took his solicitor's notes from him and scribbled down the phone number. "You do it now, and you keep it to yourself."

Charles Radford nodded. "What do I say?"

"Castleshaw Lane. That's it, you don't need to say anything other than that."

"And this is lawful?"

Waddell grinned. "What can possibly be unlawful about those two words?"

* * *

Matt and Lily drove to the village of Hade Edge in silence. By now, both of them were really worried. Something must have gone wrong, or Kate would have got in touch. Even if she'd skipped off for a couple of hours, she'd still have rung in. Matt had had enough incidents today, and he didn't need any more. But he couldn't shake the notion that something was terribly wrong.

"Next right." Lily pointed to a gap in the hedge. "Carry on along the track and it's just beyond the farm."

"Why would Ainley want a place out here?" Matt asked.

"He was seeing Caroline Waddell. It was safer for them out here, away from prying eyes," Lily said.

That made sense. But with Ainley dead, what had happened to Caroline? The canal basin and the river had been thoroughly searched but there was no sign of another body. Was it possible that she was holed up in Ainley's cottage?

Matt spotted Kate's car just before they reached the cottage. Not a good sign. There was no sign of anyone about, and the place looked deserted. The downstairs curtains were pulled tight shut, the upstairs windows were mostly boarded up.

"The place looks abandoned," Matt said. "Kate's car is still here, but where is she? We have to find her."

Lily went up to the front door and rattled the handle. "Locked, sir." She bent down and looked under the collection of flower pots beside the door. No luck. No spare key.

"If we want in, we're going to have to break the lock," Matt said.

"And we justify that how?"

Mobile in his hand, Matt was tapping in Kate's number. No response. "When have you known Kate turn her phone off?" he asked.

Lily shook her head. "Never. But she must be here somewhere. Her car is here."

Matt put his shoulder to the door and gave it a couple of hefty shoves. It sprang open almost at once.

"Kate?" Lily shouted into the gloom. "Are you okay?"

"You look down here and I'll go upstairs." Matt bounded up the stairs, and called out from the landing. "Kate! Can you hear me?"

All was quiet. He tried a few doors. Two of the bedrooms and the bathroom were empty, but the third bedroom was locked. He banged on the door and put his ear to it. He could just hear a faint groan.

"Lily! She's in here." He put his foot on the door and kicked out. The door was old, the hinges rusty, and it flew open, banging against the wall. Just inside, he saw Kate lying on the floor, barely conscious. "Get an ambulance up here!" he shouted to Lily. He lifted Kate's head from the floor. He saw blood from the back of her head on his hand. "She's been hit. She's probably concussed."

* * *

"Has she said owt?" Talbot asked. "Like who hit her?"

"No," Matt said. "She was out of it in the ambulance. They're doing a CT scan, and then we can see her. I'm going back to the hospital shortly. I'll check on Lomax again while I'm there."

"Waddell was interviewed earlier this afternoon. He was questioned about what happened to you and Paula." Talbot didn't look at all happy. Something wasn't right.

"He isn't going to wriggle out of it," Matt said. "Got proper evidence, have they?"

"Not exactly." Talbot gestured for Matt to sit down. "The serious crime squad were relying on a witness, one of Waddell's thugs who'd become disillusioned. He was going to tell them what happened and provide a video clip of a discussion between him and Waddell. The SIO has seen it himself, and he reckons it's sound. As we know from experience, once one talks, it'll open the floodgates."

Despite this good news, Talbot spoke flatly, and he kept his eyes averted from Matt's.

Matt's eyes narrowed. "What went wrong?" Not again. This was ever the way with men like Waddell.

"The witness is being kept in hiding. No one was supposed to know where. Then this afternoon he got a call on his mobile."

"A threat?"

"Not an obvious one. The caller didn't give a name, and our witness didn't recognise the number. The caller said very little." Talbot still wasn't looking at him. "I know this isn't what you want to hear, Matt. It isn't what I want to tell you either."

"How was he threatened, Talbot?"

"The caller simply told him the address of where he and his family are being kept."

Matt knew what that meant. Somehow, Waddell had found out, or been told, where the witness was staying. He groaned. Was no one or nothing safe from this man?

"I presume the leak will be investigated?"

"Yes, of course it will. But in the meantime, Leeds can't charge Waddell if they have no one prepared to testify against him."

"Can't the witness be moved? Another safe house found for him?"

"Yes, of course," Talbot said. "But we've lost his trust. He was promised absolute protection, and then this happens. He's refused to have anything to do with the Waddell case now."

"We still need to interview Waddell about our own case."

"And we will, but what evidence do we have? From what I can see, very little."

"He killed Ainley. No one else has a motive."

"Not enough, and you know it. We need someone to talk to us, Matt, and pretty quick or Waddell walks."

"Who'll interview him? I can't, Kate's in hospital. That only leaves Lily."

"In that case, it's my shout," Talbot said. "Young DC Haines can join me. We had one piece of news this afternoon. The lab confirmed that the body in the cellar is that of Amy Oliver."

Chapter 31

Kate was feeling better. The CT scan showed nothing untoward, and the painkillers had taken the edge off the headache.

"When are they letting you go home?" Zane was intent on his mobile screen. "Only I'm planning on a night out. Meeting up with Caleb in town."

"You two talking now?"

"Seems so."

Kate watched a smile lift the corners of his mouth. He'd just received a text, and it had obviously amused him.

He looked around. "Your boss is coming down the corridor. I'll get off. He asks too many questions for my liking."

"It's his job, Zane. And tonight — don't get bladdered. I'm in no state to come looking." Kate looked up as Matt entered the room and tried to smile. "Remember what I told you," she said to Zane's retreating back. "He's off round town. I'm not happy, but what can I do?"

"How are you?" Matt sat down in the chair Zane had just vacated.

"I'll live. I've been trying to piece together what happened. I arrived at the cottage and a young woman answered the door. I asked if she was Caroline and she nodded. But she looked terrified. I stepped inside and then someone else clouted me one from behind. I reckon whoever hit me was threatening her, hence her fear."

"You don't know who it was?"

"No idea. I'd expected Caroline to be alone."

"Was this her?" Matt handed her a photo that Lily had got from Caroline's mother.

Kate nodded. "At least we know that she's alive. The body at Westgate — was it Amy?"

Matt nodded. "Sadly, yes. But Caroline has disappeared again. What chance of catching her now?"

"We have to find her. We need to know what happened to Ainley. Caroline could have valuable evidence."

"We certainly need it, Kate. Waddell was arrested and taken to Leeds, but it looks like he'll walk. We'll get a chance to speak to him, but our case is flimsy at best."

"Who will do the interview?" she asked.

"Talbot and Lily. I'm desperate to give them something to work with, but without forensics or any witnesses, we're goosed."

"I'll be back tomorrow. I'll chase them up," Kate said. "There's a lot outstanding. Like the forensics from the club, and trying for a match with the packaging the money was wrapped in."

"There's no match on that, I'm afraid."

"I'll ask again, to make sure." She pulled a face. "We can't be too stringent. We want Waddell, and that means we have to keep going until we have solid evidence to present to the courts."

"For starters, I want to place Waddell at the Red Stiletto when Lomax was shot. Lomax told me he's never been there. We'll see what Waddell has to say when he's interviewed. I'm just praying we find some prints or DNA from the day of the shooting."

"Would you do me a favour?" Kate asked.

"If I can."

"Zane is off out tonight with Caleb Fletcher. I don't know what they're up to — fat chance he'd tell me anything." She hesitated. "I know it's asking a lot, but would you get uniform to keep an eye? Perhaps do a patrol past that club, see if they can clock him."

Matt nodded. "They'll be keeping an eye on that area of town anyway. Don't worry. I'll give uniform a photo of Zane. Anything happens, I'm sure they'll extricate him before too much damage is done."

* * *

"We don't upset anyone else, just Ansel," Caleb warned Zane. "She knows who's behind this. If she talks, fine. If she doesn't, she'll need a stretcher to get her out of there."

Zane had only known Caleb Fletcher for a week or two. At first, he'd thought the lad was okay, but the more he got to know him, the more he realised how much of a hothead he was. Zane had a temper, but he did know when to draw the line. Caleb went too far, and now Zane was anxious.

"We should tell the police, bro. Let them sort it."

"They won't though, will they? The cops will spin us some yarn about proof and evidence, and she'll walk. Our Kaz is terrified. These people mean business, and she's got the kid to think about. Kaz won't say owt. It's down to us. We make the bitch talk, and then we call the police."

Caleb had borrowed his mother's old car. He parked it in a side street, a few yards from the homeless shelter. It was late and the street was pitch black — the streetlight was out. Perfect. Before they got out, Caleb reached over to the back seat and picked up a baseball bat.

He grinned. "She won't argue with this little baby."

Zane was horrified. GBH was not on his programme for the night's entertainment. "You could do some real damage with that."

"Exactly! Now let's get started."

There were about six women queuing in the hallway, where another woman was dishing out tea and sandwiches from a trolley. As they passed her, she shouted at the two lads.

"You're not allowed in here, love. It's women only."

"We're expected," Caleb called back.

"Where's her office?" Zane asked.

"At the back. Down here and through the kitchen. Come on."

The office door had wood panelling on the bottom half and glass at the top. Caleb swung the bat around and brought it crashing down. The glass shattered, and splinters flew everywhere. Zane swore. This was madness.

"So where is she?" Zane asked.

The office was empty. The desk had been tidied and there was an overnight bag sitting open on top of it. They could clearly see a passport sitting on top of the contents.

"She's doing a runner!" Caleb exclaimed.

"What do you want?" The voice was female, the tone even. Both lads spun round and looked at the doorway.

"Ansel!" Caleb's face took on an expression Zane had never seen before. His eyes were wide, crazed. He had the bat grasped tight in his hand. "You're about to get one helluva beating for what you did to my sister."

"I have no idea what you're talking about. Now leave before I call the police. I know you, Caleb. You'll not get away with this. And I'll be sending the bill for the door to your mother."

"What are you running from, bitch?" Caleb spat at her.

He moved forward towards her, the bat swinging in his hand.

She spoke coolly. "I really wouldn't. Assault me, and you'll go down for a long time."

It was time for Zane to step in before things got completely out of hand. "She's right, Caleb, better to back off now before it's too late."

"It's already too late, scumbags!"

The lads stopped in their tracks. A huge man was standing in the doorway behind Ansel.

"Who are you?" Zane asked.

"Your worst nightmare." The man flexed his fists and moved forward. He took the bat from Caleb's hand as if it were a twig. All Caleb could do was stare, open-mouthed. The man swung the bat and struck him a hefty blow on the shin. Caleb fell like a stone.

Terrified, Zane took to his heels. The man might be large and tough, but he was no match for the young lad for speed. Zane ran out onto the street and carried on running. He needed to get help. God knows what state Caleb would be in by the time that brute finished with him.

When Zane reached the main road, he was gasping for breath. He chanced a look behind him. No one was following. Leaning against a shop wall, he took his mobile from his pocket and rang his sister.

"Send someone down to that homeless shelter. Caleb has been badly hurt," he panted. "Some big bloke took a baseball bat to him. Poor lad's probably dead by now." He rang off and looked round again. He should go back, try to help Caleb. He closed his eyes. Caleb was a nutter alright, but he'd found that out too late. Had the man not turned up, Zane knew he'd have done for Ansel.

Kate rang him back. "Are you okay? Where are you?"

"I'm fine. I'm going home."

"I'm home now too. The hospital discharged me an hour ago. Get a taxi, Zane, I'll pay when you get here."

Chapter 32

Day 8

"I had no idea what they planned to do," DS Kate Baxter was explaining. "He told me it was just another night out with Caleb Fletcher."

Matt cleared his throat and turned to Talbot Dyson. "She was in hospital and the lad *is* over eighteen."

Talbot sounded unimpressed. "Old enough to know better. The pair of them must have terrorised that poor woman. I'm not surprised she's gone missing. Why her, anyway?"

"Zane went to see the Fletcher family yesterday," Kate said. "They asked Karen who had imprisoned her. She told them it was Pamela Ansel."

"Why not tell us?" Talbot asked.

"I reckon Caleb didn't think we'd make it stick," Matt said.

"Sir, from the description Zane gave, I would say that the man who came to Pamela Ansel's rescue was Connor Brant. I've told Zane to come in later this morning and look at some photos."

"What's Ansel doing with Brant?" Talbot asked.

"What's Brant doing free?" Matt parried. "Yesterday he assaulted Lomax in hospital. Shouldn't he still be locked up?"

"Lomax won't press charges. He insists nothing happened, and that you lot set about Brant for no reason at all. Leeds had no choice but to release him."

"I'm getting sick of this, Talbot. We're working day and night, and still getting nowhere. Are Leeds going to lean on that witness of theirs again? We need his evidence against Waddell."

"No, lad, they've put him in another safe house but with no strings. He's scared out of his mind about his family's safety."

Talbot turned to Kate. "You well enough to be here? You can rest up for a day or so if needs be."

"I'm fine, sir. I just want to get back to normal. Sort this mess out and bring someone to book for Potter and Amy Oliver. For starters, I want to know where Ansel and Brant have got to. Zane said she had a bag packed, and her passport was in it. It looks as if the pair of them were off somewhere."

"Alert the airports. If either of them shows up, bring them in."

"Do we know how Caleb Fletcher is?" Matt asked.

"He's in the infirmary. Two broken legs. He's due to have an operation this morning," Kate said.

"I'll speak to the Fletchers again," Matt said. "Karen obviously knows more than she told us. After what has happened to her brother, she might be more inclined to talk to us now."

* * *

Matt and Kate went back to the incident room. Seated at her desk, Lily wore a big grin on her face.

"We've got something, sir," she told them excitedly. "Forensics have found some fairly fresh prints in the Red

Stiletto. They belong to Waddell, and were picked up around the bar area."

At last, something they could use. "We need that interview with Waddell sorting," Matt said.

Talbot charged into the room. "I've just been told. DC Haines, you and me will take a ride over to Leeds this afternoon. In the meantime, I'm going to sit here and read through everything you've got."

"You and Lily can do the interview, but I want to view," Matt said. "If I think you've missed something at any point, I'll send in a uniform with a note."

"Let's not have too many of them, lad. I do know my job, you know."

Kate snorted, and clapped a hand over her mouth.

Talbot put his hands on his hips. "Think that's funny, do you, Sergeant? I've been doing the job long enough. I must have learned something by now."

She shook her head. "It's not that, sir. It's the way you speak to each other, you and DI Brindle."

"I've known Matthew Brindle since he were a nipper, running around that estate of his in short pants and bare feet."

Kate and Lily exchanged a look, each willing the other not to collapse in a fit of giggles. Matt watched them, smiling. A joke at his expense, but at least it had got the two female members of his team laughing together. His smile faded. Waddell was all he could think about right now.

"Forensics come up with anything else?" Matt asked Lily.

"They are still working on the plastic bags the banknotes were in. They have some clear prints but no match on the database. They're doing more tests."

"What could Ansel have been doing with Connor Brant?" Matt wondered.

"Perhaps they're an item," Kate said. "Think about it. Ansel works for Waddell, so does Brant. It makes a sort of sense."

"I wish the rest of it did." Matt was looking at the board. "Waddell kills Ainley, or has him killed, and Ansel kills the girl in the cellar? Is that what we're going with? All this mayhem just because Waddell's wife plays away."

Lily nodded. "The scenario fits. Waddell wants to find his wife. She is known to hang around with the girls from the Red Stiletto. Ansel leans on them and in the case of Amy, things just got out of hand."

"Is Ansel up to murder?" Matt asked.

"Speak to Karen Fletcher. I'm sure she thinks so, given her experience."

"Push forensics, will you? We need more. They could have another go at that cellar. If we want to charge Ansel with Amy's murder, we need to place her in that cellar. Then the minute we catch up with her and Brant, we'll charge her." Matt looked at Lily. "Kate and I will go to the hospital and see if Caleb is able to give a statement. You had better stay here. Speak to forensics and then go over things with the super. I'll be back in a couple of hours."

Talbot looked at his watch. "We'll leave for Leeds after lunch."

* * *

When they got to the hospital, Matt decided they should split up. "See if you can find out what they've done with Caleb. If he's conscious, speak to him. I want to check in with Lomax, and bring him up to date with what's happened. He may not be aware that Waddell is in custody. He may loosen up a bit when he knows."

Kate went off to have a word with the people at reception, who told her that Caleb Fletcher was on the orthopaedic ward, recovering.

He did not deserve to have that done to him, but both he and Zane were stupid for thinking they could go it alone. Once Karen had come clean about who she had been kidnapped by, they should have come to her.

Like Lomax, Caleb Fletcher was in a side room, with a uniformed PC stationed outside. His sister was sitting with him.

"I don't need a lecture," he said, straight off. "We had no idea that thug would be there."

Kate shook her head. The lad was in a right state. Both his legs were in plaster. It'd be a while before he was on his feet again.

"You shouldn't have gone to the shelter in the first place. It got you nowhere. You're badly injured, and Ansel and friend have done one. They could be anywhere by now. Let's hope for your sake that they don't come looking — or send someone to do it for them."

"It's all my fault," Karen broke in. "I should have kept my big mouth shut."

"Or come to us before spouting off to your brother."

"I told Caleb and Zane about Ansel, but I didn't think they'd be so stupid."

Kate nodded. "You would have saved your brother a lot of grief if you'd rung me."

Kate watched Karen. Something wasn't right. The girl was nervous, ill at ease. "I wanted her punished but I didn't want Caleb hurt. I thought Caleb would tell Zane and you'd find out that way. I was hoping she'd be dragged into the nick and locked up for a bit."

"And she will be, once we catch up with her."

"But it wasn't her who imprisoned me and did this," Karen admitted finally, holding up her injured hands.

Kate and Caleb stared at her, their mouths open. Even Caleb was gobsmacked.

"You said it was!" he yelled. "You knew what I'd do, how I'd react. I don't understand what gets into you sometimes."

"Why did you lie, Karen?"

Karen looked at Kate, tears running down her cheeks. "I wanted her to know what it was like to have people chasing you. I asked that woman for help so many times, and she always laughed at me. It was down to her that I got involved with that bloody club. When things got really bad, she wouldn't even give me a bed for the night, just turned me out onto the street."

"You could have come home," Caleb said.

"I might have done, but then I got that phone call. Some woman I didn't know wanted to give me cash for information about Caroline. I'd nothing to lose, so I agreed. Instead of bothering Ansel anymore, I asked Amy if she'd put me up for a couple of nights."

"Amy and Caroline were living at the house on Westgate?"

Karen nodded. "Him too — that Ainley bloke who owned the club."

"Did you know that the woman who contacted you was working for Caroline's husband?" Kate asked.

"Yes, she told me. She said there'd be more money once he got her home."

"Do you know who she is?"

"No."

She was telling the truth. What had happened to Caleb had shaken her. Karen was staring at her brother like a frightened child, shocked out of her compulsion to lie.

"It was Caroline's husband who had your brother hurt?" Kate asked.

"No," said Caleb. "That was down to some huge bloke with Ansel. An ugly brute, thickset with a bald head and beady little eyes."

"Connor Brant," Karen said. "He came to the club all the time. Made Lomax as nervous as hell."

Kate nodded. "Take my word for it, Caleb. He worked for Caroline's husband. Caroline herself worked at the club for a while. Didn't Brant ever see her there?"

"No. She spotted him once and hid. After that that, she left. I got the impression that her and Ainley were planning to do one."

"Didn't she realise how dangerous it was for her to work there?" Kate asked.

"She'd no idea about her old man's involvement with the place. She wanted to be there because of Ainley. He owned it. And Lomax had no idea who she was. As far as he was concerned, Caroline was just Ainley's latest."

"Why did Brant visit the club, Karen? Do you know what he and Lomax spoke about?" Kate asked.

"It was about the money." This surprised Kate. "Lisa told Amy that Lomax put the money he got from Brant through the till. With the bar, and particularly the casino, the club made a mint. All I know is that the pair used to swap bags full of the stuff every time Brant visited."

Money laundering. They'd suspected that, but now they had a witness who'd seen money changing hands in the club. That must be what happened to the money from the bank robbery. The amount stolen was huge. They must still be processing it.

"We need this in a statement, Karen. These people can't be allowed to get away with what they've done."

Karen looked at her brother. "I daren't grass. Those people aren't just petty crooks. They'd kill me."

"I know they're killers, Karen, which is why they need putting away," Kate said. "Until that happens, while they remain free, you and your family are in real danger."

* * *

Martin Lomax saw Matt come in and groaned. He leant back on his pillows. "I can't talk now, I've got a headache."

"I won't stay long," Matt said. He saw get well cards on the beside cabinet, and someone had brought flowers. "People are missing you," Matt said. "Heard from Waddell?"

"No idea who you mean."

"He's in custody. The serious crime squad in Leeds have got hold of him. I don't think he'll wriggle out of it so easily this time."

"You have nothing. You'll get no witnesses. No one is going to risk having Waddell's thugs on their backs. Even if you do bang him up, the threat doesn't go away. He has a bloody long memory."

"He is going down, along with everyone connected to him. Waddell has killed people, and we are gathering evidence to prove it. It's only a matter of time before someone sees sense and gives a statement. There's another of his victims in here, by the way. How many more people have to suffer before someone sees sense and puts a stop to him?"

Lomax shook his head. "It'll never happen."

"We can prove that he was at your club the day you were assaulted."

"So were any number of people."

"But you said he wasn't there. You don't know Waddell, remember?" Matt smiled. "Have you heard from that lad of yours?"

"He's on his way back. Once I'm out of here, the two of us are going away. Somewhere that thug can't find us."

"I feel sorry for you, Lomax. You'll be looking over your shoulder and running for the rest of your life."

"Get out of here and leave me alone, copper. I'm keeping silent. My choice. You can't force a statement out of me, but Waddell can blow my head off."

Lomax wasn't going to change his mind. For now, Matt would have to accept that. "The offer to talk still stands." He went out.

Matt was back in the car waiting for Kate when his mobile rang. It was Graham Harwood from forensics.

"I think we've got something. Can you pop in sometime this morning, and I'll explain?"

"Sounds interesting."

"It's something that should have been picked up before, so I apologise."

Matt's curiosity was aroused. "Okay, Graham. I'm at the hospital at the moment, but I should be there within the hour."

Kate had arrived back at the car. "Karen Fletcher is a piece of work, she really is. Caleb getting injured like that has shaken her up alright, but getting a statement out of her is something else."

"Same with Lomax."

"Money laundering is at the bottom of this," she said. "The Red Stiletto is being used to do it. No doubt half the clubs in Huddersfield as well."

Matt nodded. "And many further afield. Waddell isn't just a local villain, his reach is far and wide."

Chapter 33

Graham Harwood ushered Matt and Kate into his lab. "I'm sorry about this. It shouldn't have happened. The information should have been with you a lot sooner."

"What information, Graham?" Matt asked. "What we're looking for is cast iron proof of Jack Waddell's guilt. Is that what you're talking about?"

The scientist gave him a funny look. "No, sorry. What we have doesn't concern Waddell at all."

"Then don't beat yourself up about it," Matt said.

"You gave us a number of bank notes in plastic bags. There were four of them in total, and we tested them thoroughly for prints. As expected, we found some. Those of Karen Fletcher and one other."

That made sense. "The unknown woman who gave her money, then locked her up," Kate said.

"Well, she isn't so unknown anymore."

This was good news. The woman, whoever she was, was a link to Waddell.

"True, the prints weren't in the database. But at that time, we hadn't checked them against the prints from this current case. When we did, we found a match."

"Who do they belong to, Graham?" Matt asked, impatient. Whoever this person was had imprisoned and tortured Karen, and could be responsible for the body in the cellar.

"Francine Potter."

Kate blinked. "Say that again. Are you sure?"

"Positive. Her prints were found at the house in Westgate, and they match the ones on the plastic wrappers from the bank. She definitely handled that money."

"Are there any more unidentified prints in the pipeline?" Matt asked.

"We're still looking at those from the Potter murder. There was very little forensics, and the residue on the cupboard door you know about. But there is a set of unidentified prints. They may belong to your killer. And they definitely don't match any in the database."

Matt and Kate returned to the car in silence.

"What now?" Kate said.

"Francine Potter — who else? But I have to say I'm surprised."

"Now I think about it, I'm not, actually" Kate said. "She's greedy. She'd have taken Potter for every penny if she could, and she did work at the Red Stiletto for a while, Salter told us that much. She's not stupid. Like Karen, Francine will have seen the money laundering going on."

"But to kill and then burn the body? That's what I can't get my head around."

"She may well have had help. Lomax, maybe? Who knows. Hopefully this one will talk to us, and give us something we can use."

It took less than ten minutes to reach Francine's house. Her red sports car was in the drive. She was at home.

She opened the door to them with the familiar scowl. "You lot again. What now?"

"We want you to come down to the station, Francine. Answer some questions," Matt said.

"No can do." She nodded at her son, standing just behind her. "There's no one to take care of him."

"No matter. We'll get someone." Matt turned to Kate. "Get onto Social Services, and tell them what we need."

"You can't do this! What do you think I've done, for pity's sake? This isn't right. I've done nowt."

* * *

It was Melissa and a colleague who came to Francine's. Matt should have realised. Melissa worked with the emergency team. They would take the boy away and look after him until the interview was over. Although, given the evidence they had, Matt doubted that Francine would be released anytime soon. He told Melissa as much on the quiet.

Francine Potter sat with the duty solicitor in an interview room, tapping her manicured fingernails on the desktop. Nerves, perhaps?

Matt and Kate entered the room and sat facing them. "Do you know why you are here?" Matt asked.

"Haven't a bloody clue. But I need to get off soon. My lad doesn't like strangers."

"Does the name Amy Oliver mean anything to you?" Kate asked.

"Who?"

"Come on, Francine. Don't mess us about. We know you knew Amy. You worked at that club like she did. Pay well, did it? Dancing, serving drinks — or perhaps you worked in the casino?"

"I did a bit of dancing. I was good too. Martin said I had a future."

"So what went wrong?"

Francine looked down. "I got pregnant. Couldn't carry on after that, could I?"

"Are you talking about Ronald Potter's child?" Kate asked.

"Yes, of course. I met him in the pub one night on my day off, and we clicked. But I didn't know him then, did I?"

"I bet a lot of girls who work in that club get themselves pregnant. Doesn't Lomax help them sort it out?"

"Martin Lomax has paid for a lot of abortions. He has an arrangement with a private clinic. But that wasn't for me."

"You do have a heart." Kate smiled. "Pity it wasn't much in evidence when you tortured and killed that poor girl, Amy."

"That wasn't me!" Francine screamed. "How can you think something so gross? I wouldn't know where to start! I was looking after her."

"In that case, I wouldn't want you looking after one of mine," Kate said.

"Were you paid to do this, Francine?" Matt asked.

"I was supposed to be, once I'd handed Amy over. Caroline's husband wanted her back. He was desperate. I had no idea where she'd gone, but Amy knew. She and Caroline were close. When Amy was on her own, she asked me stay with her for a few nights. She was scared, I think. Ronald had taken our son away for the weekend, so I was free. I met Amy at the club and gave her a lift back to Westgate. I didn't know it then, but Caroline had already left with Ainley, and Karen had disappeared."

"What was Caroline's husband's name?" Matt asked.

"Jack."

"Did he ever come to Westgate?"

"Yes."

Why hadn't forensics picked up any evidence of Waddell's presence? There had to be a trace, surely.

"What was he like, Caroline's husband?" Kate asked.

"A weird one. Big. Ugly. Not at all what I expected."

"Was this him?" Kate showed her a photo of Connor Brant.

"Yes."

So Francine had mistakenly thought Brant was Waddell. "Did anyone else come with him?"

"There was some bloke waiting outside. His driver perhaps. He sat in the car, smoking and looking across at the house."

"But he never went inside?"

Francine shook her head.

"Did he see Amy?"

"No. I don't know what happened that particular night. She never came home, and I never saw her again."

"Did you know that Amy had been killed?" Matt asked.

"Not then, but I did wonder later."

"Did you tell Ronald about this?" Matt asked.

"No. I didn't see the point. The house went on the market, so I presumed everything was okay."

"Weren't you worried about Amy?" Kate said. "Didn't you think to contact us? Report her missing?"

Francine shook her head. "I thought she must have told them about Caroline and they'd paid her off. I thought she was keeping away, because I never got a penny."

Kate looked at Matt. That didn't fit with the evidence. Her prints were on those bags.

"Caroline's husband contacted you again. Tell us about that," Kate said.

"Where did you get that from?" Francine seemed genuinely surprised. "I've not heard anything from that day to this. That bloke was seriously odd, and I don't want him anywhere near, thank you. I've got a kid to protect."

Chapter 34

Matt and Kate were on their way back to the incident room. "What do you think?" Matt asked.

"She admitted something," Kate said. "As to the rest, I think she's telling the truth. And if you consider what we know about Waddell's relationship with Brant, it fits. Brant does all the dirty work."

"It doesn't help us with who killed Amy, or Potter, or who held Karen captive and bashed you on the head. We're still nowhere." Matt sighed.

"I realise that. We're seriously running out of suspects, aren't we?" Kate said.

"Then there's the problem of the fingerprints, the ones on the plastic bags Karen had. There is no doubt about it, they're definitely Francine's."

"Let's ask her," Kate said. "Give her a break, then we start again. We'll get to the bottom of that one and see where it takes us." She went to her desk and sat down, frowning.

Matt smiled at her. "You were impressive in there. Shame you're not going up against Waddell. I think you'd give him a run for his money."

Apart from a couple of uniforms, the incident room was empty. Talbot and Lily must be having a bite to eat before going to Leeds. Would he make it in time? Matt wondered. Should he even try? He decided to see how things went with Francine.

Kate looked up. "I was knocked on the head at about lunchtime. Lily has left me a note. She's checked, and Francine was doing a stint at her son's nursery at the time. She has an alibi."

Matt buried his head in his hands. So Francine wasn't the person who attacked Kate. "Are you sure you didn't hear a voice? Catch even a glimpse of whoever hit you?"

"I was too taken up with finding Caroline," she said. "One minute, relief, and the next . . . bang. Sorry, sir, I know that doesn't help."

"Okay. Francine has had long enough. Let's see what else she has to say."

The two detectives returned to the interview room. This time Kate even managed to smile at the young woman.

"You made a mistake trusting Caroline's husband. We believe that you didn't kill anyone, Francine," Kate said. "But we have some damaging evidence that puts you in the frame for another kidnap. The particularly nasty kidnap of a young woman who was tortured and suffered injuries."

Francine winced.

"I'd never hurt anyone," she said. "What evidence?"

"Someone gave a young woman a lot of money in new notes, allegedly in exchange for information. They were part of a robbery carried out a while ago. Can you explain how your fingerprints came to be on those plastic money bags?" Kate asked.

Francine shook her head. "I don't know what you're talking about."

Kate sifted through her paperwork and presented Francine with another photo. "This is what they look like."

"Ronald had some like that in the office safe. The last time he gave me money for our son, he paid me in new notes."

"And he took them from a bag like this?"

Francine nodded.

"When was this?" Matt asked.

"Last week. I was broke and went to the office. We got into a row, and he ended up opening the safe and giving me the notes. Salter went berserk. Kept going on about how sooner or later I'd bankrupt the place. She said the money was a deposit from a client, and she was supposed to take it to the bank later."

"What did Ronald say to her?"

"He apologised, and said he'd replace what he gave me at lunchtime."

"So you did touch the bags?" Matt asked.

"Yes, a couple of them for certain. But there were about ten in there."

* * *

"Salter!" Matt said. "Arrange for Francine to write a statement and then she can go."

"Do we pick Salter up?" Kate asked.

"Oh yes. We'll try the estate agents first, then her home address. This could be the breakthrough we've been looking for."

"Let's hope so. There's no one else left," Kate said. "I wonder how the super and Lily are doing with Waddell?"

He smiled grimly. "We need to move. We get a confession from Salter, they'll be able to finish Waddell."

Chapter 35

Mary Salter was not at her desk. Instead, they found the part-timer, Julie.

"She said she didn't feel well. All the strain and stress of the week has finally got to her I reckon."

"Would you open the safe, please?" Matt asked.

"Why? What are you looking for?"

"We're investigating a murder case, Julie," Kate said. "Just do as DI Brindle asks."

"It isn't locked. There are some documents in there that I need this afternoon so Mary left it open."

Matt pulled open the door and looked inside. There were several bundles of paperwork, and there on the bottom shelf, he saw the plastic bags containing the banknotes. "Do you know where these came from?"

"I think someone paid Mary a deposit on a rental property. She keeps meaning to go to the bank with them."

"There's a lot of money here." Matt reckoned it must be about three thousand pounds. With the two they'd got from Karen's room, that made five in all. Was that the amount Waddell had paid for information about his wife?

"This is evidence," he said. "We'll bag it up, and then I want you to lock the safe until one of our officers comes to collect it. Do you understand, Julie?"

She nodded.

"Where does Mary Salter live?" Kate asked.

"Blackstone Road, number thirty. Lovely old house it is. Far too big for a woman on her own, but she doesn't seem to mind."

They returned to the car.

"How far?" Kate asked.

"Through Marsden and off the Slaithwaite Road. It should take us about five minutes. But first, I want a quick word with the station, and then Graham at forensics."

Matt instructed the officers who would collect the money to take it straight to Graham Harwood. He asked him to check it for fingerprints, particularly any belonging to Jack Waddell or Mary Salter.

Salter's car was parked in the drive. Julie was right. The house was a large stone detached, with ivy covering the front.

"Cost a bob or two," Kate remarked. "She's only an admin in the local estate agents. Wonder how she managed to come by this?"

"Let's not jump to conclusions. She could have inherited the money."

Matt knocked at the door. They had to wait several minutes before she answered.

She stood frowning at them. "What now? I'm tired, I need to rest after everything that's gone on."

"We'd like a word," Matt said.

"Make it quick. I was having a lie-down."

"We can do it here or down at the station. Your choice."

Reluctantly, she led them inside. "I can't see what I can do for you. I've told you everything I know."

"You can tell us where Caroline Waddell is for starters," Kate said.

Salter stared long and hard at them. "I don't know anyone of that name."

"We think you do. We think her husband hired you to find her."

"Nonsense! I have no idea who she is. Who told you that?"

"Caroline was one of the young women you allowed to stay in the house on Westgate. The other one, Amy Oliver, was murdered there. The evidence is building. We have sent the money in your safe to be fingerprinted."

"You can't prove a thing. I was simply doing those girls a favour. This is what I get for helping out. Wish I hadn't bothered now." She turned and stalked off into the house, Matt and Kate following.

"How does Waddell contact you?"

"I don't know who you mean. I don't know the man."

Matt had heard enough. "I want you to come down to the station. We have more questions, and you'll be needing a solicitor."

* * *

"Will she talk?" Kate asked Matt.

He shrugged. "I'm not sure. It depends how scared she is of Waddell."

"Anything from the lab?"

"Graham promised to be as quick as he can," he said.

Kate checked the clock. "I'll give him a ring."

One of the uniformed officers called out to Matt. "Sir! DC Haines rang in about twenty minutes ago. They aren't getting anywhere with Waddell. She says he's running rings around them."

They needed evidence badly.

"They match!" Kate shouted triumphantly, replacing the phone. "Graham found Salter's prints on those bags, along with Waddell's. Salter definitely handled them."

"Let's face her with it. Get a search warrant organised," he told the uniform. "I want her home gone over with a fine toothcomb."

Ready to go, Matt grabbed the case file.

"How d'you think she'll react?" Kate asked.

"Knowing the kind of woman Mary Salter is, I think she'll try for a deal. There's no way she'll want to go to prison for any length of time."

"But if she killed Amy, our hands are tied."

"We'll see. That may have been down to Brant, or even Waddell himself."

Mary Salter looked decidedly nervous as the detectives entered the room.

"We have found your prints and those of Jack Waddell on those money bags. He handled them when he passed them to you as payment for information, didn't he, Mary?"

"No comment."

Matt could see this was merely bravado. The woman was nervous. Her hands were shaking. Kate saw it too.

"If you speak to us, it'll help your case further down the line," Kate urged.

Salter narrowed her eyes and regarded the DS closely. "If I explain what happened, will you release me?"

"That depends on what you tell us," Kate said.

Salter leaned toward her solicitor and whispered to him.

"Okay. What if I tell you where Caroline is?" she said.

"That's a start," Matt said, "but there's a lot more to clear up."

"Caroline is still at the cottage at Hade Edge. She's locked in the cellar. I kept her at mine after you found her," she nodded at Kate. "But that was too risky, so I took her back."

Matt gestured to the uniformed officer seated in a corner. "Get someone up there. Bring her back."

"You have to understand how things were," Salter began. "Caroline was living in one of our houses, the one on Westgate. Her husband was looking for her. Some woman who works for him was doing the rounds of the agents, asking if Caroline had approached them. I recognised her photo."

"What was she offering?" Kate asked, and set down a photo of Pamela Ansel in front of her.

"A down payment, with more to follow once Waddell got his wife back. She assured me that it was just a newlyweds tiff. She told me he had booked an expensive holiday and didn't want them to miss out on it."

"Was this her?" Kate asked.

"Yes."

Kate nodded. "So you agreed to help."

"Not straight away. I negotiated a little. Initially, he paid me five grand. But things went awry when Caroline ran off with that Ainley bloke. That put me in a right predicament, I can tell you. She threatened me." Salter tapped the photo of Ansel. "Said I didn't want to find myself on the wrong side of Waddell, things could get out of hand." She wiped a tear from her eye. "That was when Ronald got killed. I still don't know why that happened. I thought it might be a warning to me."

"Do you know who killed him?" Kate asked.

"I'm not sure. Waddell has this henchman. It could have been him."

"Tell us what happened to Amy," Matt urged.

"I had no choice. You can see that, can't you? I had Waddell on my back and nowhere to run. I asked Amy where Caroline was, but she kept insisting that she didn't know. I knew she was lying, so I'm sorry to say I hit her. I'm not proud of it. She was weeping, terrified of what I'd do next. I was very angry. Waddell had rung me, threatening all sorts. Amy wasn't the only one who was terrified that night. I took another swipe at her. Not hard, but she fell backwards and cracked her head on the staircase. She didn't get up. I really thought I'd killed her."

"Why didn't you call for help?" Matt asked.

"*He* turned up. Waddell. He saw what I'd done and said he'd sort it. There was nothing I could do."

"Waddell usually has someone with him — that minder you mentioned," Kate said.

"Not that night he didn't, he was alone. He dragged Amy into the kitchen, and then I heard her scream. I realised that I hadn't killed her after all. I went in after them, and what I saw turned my stomach. Waddell had his back to me, so I stood against the wall and listened. He was hitting her, asking where Caroline was. I wanted to help, but what could I do? He had a knife."

"Waddell killed her?" Matt asked.

"Yes. He went too far. He beat her to a pulp, she lost consciousness and couldn't speak at all. Then he stuck the knife into her. It must have got her heart, there was blood everywhere. I was in shock, but I had the presence of mind to take a photo with my phone. The light from the hallway was behind me, so the quality isn't bad. I thought that if things got out of hand, I could use it against him. You'll find it in my bag."

"What did Waddell do then? Did he threaten you?" Matt asked.

"I ran. I'm not proud of what I did that night, but I wasn't going to take the blame. I got out of that house as fast as I could."

"And Karen? Why imprison and hurt her?"

"Because Waddell wouldn't let up. He had my number. He kept on threatening me, again and again. I either found Caroline or ended up dead myself."

"Why not use the photo on your phone as evidence?" Matt asked.

"I worried that it wouldn't stand up. People can create anything with fancy software these days. I was terrified. Waddell isn't someone you mess with."

"Where did you keep Karen Fletcher imprisoned?"

"An empty old house in Marsden. We have a lot on our books," she added with a sly smile. "I kept her in the cellar, until she escaped. I didn't want to hurt her, but I was desperate after all Waddell's threats. He's not someone you cross. He said if I didn't find Caroline, it would be me next."

"You never thought to look at the cottage at Hade Edge, the one Ainley rented?" Kate asked.

"I didn't know about it until after Ronald died and I was sorting through his stuff. I found a note in his drawer about Ainley going to view the cottage. I went up there and waited. I saw Caroline there one day. That was when I put pressure on Waddell for more money. I was able to tell him that I knew where Caroline was, and how much I wanted."

Kate gave a faint smile. "Did he agree?"

"He had no choice. He wanted his wife back."

Matt didn't doubt she was telling the truth. This woman was selfish and greedy. But they needed solid evidence, something that put him at the house on Westgate. Forensics had been over it and found nothing. Someone had done a superb job of cleaning up. But what about his clothing from that night? There could be traces of Amy's blood on that, or in his car.

"You have to protect me," Mary Salter was saying. "That's what you people do, isn't it? Provide new identities and a safe house?"

"We have your statement, Mary," Kate said. "We'll look at your phone records and then we'll talk again." Kate looked at her. "It was you who hit me, wasn't it?"

"Sorry. I recognised you, and realised you must know the truth. I regretted it afterwards."

* * *

Matt had to speak to Talbot. The super needed to know what they had discovered. There was no time to get to the interview himself, so he rang him.

"You're fortunate, I've just sorted a break. Tell you what, he's a cool bugger alright. He's trying to run rings around us. And given that we've got nowt, it's working."

"I want a warrant to search Waddell's house and take his car. We have a witness who saw him stab and kill Amy Oliver. She even took a photo. It's not bad quality either. She says he was covered in blood. There has to be a trace somewhere. When we find one, we'll be able to nail him. He contacted Salter by phone. He'll have a pay-as-you-go stashed somewhere. We need to find it."

There was no reply. Talbot was considering this.

"Okay, go for it," he said at last. "We'll resume the interview tomorrow. I hope to God you're right. I don't want to give the bastard the satisfaction of walking free again. Leeds couldn't make their case stick, so we have to be absolutely sure with ours."

"Graham Harwood says he'll work flat out on anything we give him."

"You have to find it first. Get that warrant and organise the search." Talbot ended the call.

"The uniforms that went up to the Hade Edge cottage have found Caroline. She's in the infirmary for now," Kate told him. "I hope she's okay. Salter is a hard woman."

"I wonder what tale she will have for us."

"Nothing too grim, I hope," Kate said. "She may well know what happened to Ainley. And if so, will she give evidence?"

Chapter 36

Day 9

Matt woke the following morning to the sound of his mobile beeping. It was a text from Kate. She'd been at Waddell's house at Ogden Moor all night, and they had found something.

Ring me asap.

He did so at once. "What have you got? Matt yawned. He'd lain awake most of the night going over the possibilities.

"Forensics have gone over his car. It has been cleaned several times — the bloke must have done it every other day. Buuut," she drew the word out, "they picked up a minute trace of blood in the boot. It's with Graham now. If it turns out to belong to Amy, then we've done it."

"Good work. What about the mobile?" Matt asked, fully awake now.

"We're still looking. Currently we're tearing the summerhouse apart. By the way, Brant and Ansel were apprehended in the early hours. They were on a ferry, on their way to Holland. But there's something else. Salter thinks Potter was killed as a warning to her. Waddell usually got Brant to do his dirty work, but the day Potter was stabbed, he was in London with Waddell. It can't have been him."

Matt rubbed his head. If not Brant, then who? "I'll come and join you soon. If you get anything else, ring me."

The Potter problem aside, the rest of it was good news. If there was any justice, the blood alone would put Waddell away — provided it was Amy's. But the villain was slippery and could afford the best lawyers. Despite all that had been done, they still needed more.

His mother popped her head around the door. "Breakfast is on the kitchen table. You work too hard, Matthew. You need a break. I'll have a word with Talbot, make him understand what you've been through."

"I'm not a child, Ma. It's police work, remember? And we're very close to cracking the case."

"The one involving Jack?" she asked.

"I'm afraid so. If we get it right, he'll be charged with murder."

"And to think I dated him. I'll never forgive myself for being taken in so easily."

"He plays a good game. Don't give yourself a hard time, Ma."

All Matt could do was wait for the results from forensics. A text from Talbot told him that Ansel and Brant had also been taken to Leeds for questioning. Matt decided to visit the hospital, bring Martin Lomax up to speed and see if Caroline was able to talk. The news of Waddell's imminent arrest might change Lomax's mind about giving a statement.

"I'm leaving, Ma!" he shouted down the hallway.

"Don't be too late tonight. We're having guests."

Matt groaned. That was all he needed.

Martin Lomax was still where Matt had left him. "How are you doing?"

Lomax grimaced. "No better for seeing you. I still have nothing to say."

"I wanted you to be the first to know that the net is closing in on your friend Waddell. Today we will have the cast iron proof we need to put him away for a long time."

"And that interests me why, exactly?"

"You'll be free of him," Max said.

Lomax burst out laughing. "You think it's that easy? You have no idea, do you, copper? Lock him up, throw away the key, but you won't stop him. Waddell is an evil bastard, someone you don't cross. Ever!"

"We'll protect you and your son. I've told you that."

"Not well enough. And what about Brant?"

"He is under lock and key too."

Matt watched the expression on Lomax's face change. Was he considering the offer? "We know he killed Amy Oliver, one of your ex-dancers. We have a witness, and forensic evidence."

"So why are you wasting time with me? What haven't you got?"

"A mobile phone, a pay-as-you-go. It'll be hidden somewhere, but Waddell's property up on the moor is huge."

"It won't be there." Lomax sounded certain.

Matt looked at him. "You think he'll have destroyed it?"

"No." Lomax put his hand under his pillow and produced a mobile, wrapped in a plastic bag. "Here. This is his."

Matt stared at him. "I don't understand. How did you get hold of this?"

"The day Brant tried to kill me, Waddell left us. He had a pain, he said, indigestion or something, and would wait in the car. He was rattled, kept rubbing his chest. He pulled out the contents of his breast pocket and put them on the bar. A lighter, his wallet and two mobiles. I'd seen him use one often, but the other was old. I was sure it was important. As Brant turned to watch him go, I slipped it into my trouser pocket. It was a spur of the moment thing, I'd no idea what I'd do with it. But if it gets that bastard off my tail, take it."

Matt took the phone from him. "Thank you. Is your son back here now?"

Lomax nodded.

"I'll arrange protection for you both. Are you prepared to give a statement? Appear in court and give evidence?"

"Don't push it, copper."

Next, he went to see Caroline. She was sitting in an armchair in a private room with a police guard. When Matt went in, she shrank back into the chair. The poor girl was afraid of her own shadow.

"I'm from the police," he said with a reassuring smile. "I have a few questions. Do you feel up to it?"

"I'm very tired, but I'll try to help."

"Do you know what happened to Paul Ainley?"

At the mention of Ainley's name, she burst into tears. "He went to the supermarket to get some food. He never came back. They must have got him. He'd never have willingly told them where I was. They'll have hurt him. I don't want to think about it. I read in the paper how he was found."

"Do you know what your bag was doing in the boot?"

"Jack will have done that. He had every intention of killing me too. If you found the bag, you'd think I was killed along with Paul."

"Your husband wanted you dead?" Matt asked.

"Yes. You don't run out on a man like him. If he'd found me . . ." She buried her head in her hands.

"You stayed at the house on Westgate with your friends from the club, is that right?"

"Yes, but it was too risky. That was why Paul found us the cottage at Hade Edge."

"Do you mind if I send someone to take your fingerprints? It's just to rule them out. We found a number of different prints at Westgate, but one set has yet to be identified."

Her eyes were wide. "No! I don't want that."

"I'm afraid you don't have much choice. We're looking for a killer. A man was stabbed in the kitchen of that house, and we have unidentified prints."

Caroline was staring out of the window. Matt wasn't sure if she was even listening.

Finally she spoke. She sounded utterly broken. "It was me. I'd had enough. Jack never gives up. I knew he would pursue me until the bitter end. I went to Westgate to pick up some of my stuff. The man was there. I asked him what he wanted, and he got annoyed. He said I was trespassing."

Potter couldn't have known anything about Mary Salter's arrangement with the girls.

"I panicked. I'd taken to carrying a knife in my bag for protection against Jack's thugs. I don't know what got into me. Seconds later, the man was on the floor, bleeding out."

"You left him there? You didn't call for help?" Matt asked.

"No. I heard voices outside and I ran out of the back door and along the lane behind the row. I didn't pass anyone. I'd parked my car by the shops on the corner."

Matt looked at the officer standing guard. "No one gets in or out, and don't let her out of your sight."

Back in his car, Matt rang Kate and told her about the mobile Lomax had given him. "I'll get it to forensics, and then you can break the good news to Waddell." Then he told her about Caroline and Potter.

"Do you want me to ring the super?" Kate asked.

"Yes. Tell him I'll stop the search now. Oh, and get someone round to the hospital to fingerprint Caroline. We still need to confirm that it is her prints on that knife."

* * *

"I was about to ring you." Graham Harwood was smiling. "The blood in Waddell's car matches Amy Oliver's. We also found a heavy duty garden waste incinerator in the shed. We've taken it for analysis."

That was good news. Waddell killed Amy, took her back to his and tried to destroy her body by burning it. What Matt didn't understand was why he'd taken the remains back to the house on Westgate. Perhaps he planned to pin the lot on Caroline if things went wrong — the murders of both Potter and Amy. Matt handed Graham the phone Lomax had given him. "It's the mobile Waddell used to contact the people he put pressure on. See what you can find."

"It's a good result, Matt. You and your team should be pleased with yourselves."

"We'll get Waddell for Amy's murder. No doubt he ordered the killing of Ainley too. Caroline has just confessed to killing Potter. But it bugs me that Waddell walks on the one charge I really want him for."

"What he did to you and your colleague?" Graham asked.

"What he did to Paula was to kill her. Or had someone do it for him. I favour Connor Brant, now that I know how Waddell operates."

"There's still time for one of his people to talk. You know what it's like. You get one and the floodgates open."

Matt shook his head. "We can only hope so." His mobile rang. It was Kate.

"Something has happened, sir." Her voice was flat. She didn't sound at all happy.

"What do you mean?" he asked. "What's happened?"

"It's Waddell."

"That bloody brief of his hasn't come up with some fairy tale and got him out on bail, has he?" Matt rubbed his neck. He could feel the tension building. It was one step forward and two back all the time with Waddell.

"No, nothing like that."

She fell silent, while Matt's imagination did overtime. "Come on, Kate. Do I have to guess?"

"He's dead, sir. A massive heart attack, sometime during the night. The officer went to wake him this morning and he was laid out under the blanket, stiff as a board."

Matt closed his eyes. "Didn't they check on him during the night?"

"Yes. The log says he was asleep."

"But he wasn't, was he? The bloody villain had gone and died on us. What's Talbot said?"

"He appears to have taken it in his stride. Reckons it'll save the taxpayer a fortune. No trial, you see."

Matt didn't know what to think. Part of him was okay with Waddell being dead — just a pity it hadn't happened sooner. But he'd wanted to see the villain squirm in court, and justice be served.

"Waddell is dead. Heart attack," he said to Graham Harwood. "Anything you find that implicates Connor Brant, let us know."

"You okay with it? Him dying like that?"

"I have no choice, have I? One thing, though. It'll be easier to lean on his people, now that he's gone and Brant locked up."

Epilogue

The dining room at Brindle Hall looked splendid. When Evelyn Brindle put on a dinner party, she did it in style.

"Who is coming?" Matt asked.

"Everyone, Matthew. It's about time you socialised a little. I've invited the Cassons. Their daughter Annabel is still unattached."

"Mother! Please don't play matchmaker. I'm more than capable of making my own arrangements."

"You haven't taken a young lady out since Melissa. That must change. You have responsibilities. This place needs an heir."

"That's a bit old-fashioned, Ma. Sarah has kids. Her Henry could run this place as well as anyone else."

"Henry is not a Brindle."

He smiled. "It's only a name."

"Talbot is here. Go and meet him."

"Have you invited anyone else from the station?" he asked.

"Yes. I know how important your colleagues are to you. I've asked Lily and that new woman, Kate Baxter, plus Carlisle and his assistant, Beckwith."

Matt reckoned Beckwith wouldn't think much of being called Carlisle's assistant.

Matt's team arrived together. Talbot had made a special effort and brought flowers and chocolates for Evelyn. He took her arm and ushered her into the conservatory.

Kate grinned. "Keen, isn't he?"

"Yes, but he's harmless. And Ma does like him, despite what she says."

"I had no idea you lived in such luxury." Kate spun around. "This place is wonderful, so full of history."

Matt smiled. "We've got history oozing out of every pore. But until we opened the place to the public, we were broke."

"Your mother has a title — Lady Brindle. Will that pass to you one day?"

"Thankfully, no. My father was knighted for his services to industry."

"Your mum had a narrow escape with Waddell. The super is very much the softer option I'd say."

Lily interrupted. "Now that he's dead and Brant is in custody, we can't stop Waddell's people talking. The money laundering scam has been scuppered. The Red Stiletto is closed. One bloke came forward and talked about what happened to you and your sergeant. We have him in custody, and he's prepared to make a statement. You might get justice after all."

"I don't know about justice. I'll settle for being able to draw a line under it."

Lily nudged him. "There's a glamourous blonde ogling you, sir."

The hall had filled up with his mother's guests. The girl Lily referred to was Annabelle Casson.

Matt felt his mobile vibrate in his jacket pocket. His mother strictly forbade phones on evenings like this. He gave it a furtive glimpse. It was Graham Harwood. Matt went into the study and locked the door.

"What have you got, Graham?"

"The prints on the knife that killed Potter. They do belong to Caroline Waddell."

"Thanks for letting me know. She did confess and she's in custody. I'll tell Talbot." He went back to the gathering.

"Where's Talbot?"

Lily nodded at the patio area outside the conservatory. "He's got your mother in a clinch. No way can you interrupt now."

THE END

Thank you for reading this book. If you enjoyed it please leave feedback on Amazon, and if there is anything we missed or you have a question about then please get in touch. The author and publishing team appreciate your feedback and time reading this book.

Our email is office@joffebooks.com

www.joffebooks.com

ALSO BY HELEN H. DURRANT

CALLADINE & BAYLISS MYSTERIES
DEAD WRONG
DEAD SILENT
DEAD LIST
DEAD LOST
DEAD & BURIED
DEAD NASTY
DEAD JEALOUS
DEAD BAD

DI GRECO
DARK MURDER
DARK HOUSES
DARK TRADE
DARK ANGEL

DI MATT BRINDLE
HIS THIRD VICTIM
THE OTHER VICTIM

35844170R00141

Printed in Poland
by Amazon Fulfillment
Poland Sp. z o.o., Wrocław